DEAD AIM

DEAD AIM

by Collin Wilcox

Random House : New York

This book is dedicated to
Addie Gilbert,
with the deepest thanks

DEAD AIM

1

Friedman slumped into my visitor's chair, sighing deeply and shaking his head sadly as he sailed a departmental memo across my desk.

"At age forty-six," he said heavily, "I've finally gotten used to the idea of being Jewish. When I was a kid, I used to get into fights about being Jewish—most of which I lost. When I was a struggling patrolman who never wanted to be a cop anyhow, I was edgy about being a Jew. When I didn't advance in the department, I decided it was discrimination. I finally figured out, though, that the problem was really two kids, both in diapers at the same time, plus a wife who was too pooped to do much at night but sleep. So eventually I made detective, then detective sergeant. Then, lo, I made lieutenant. The kids, meanwhile, are growing up, and Clara is pinching me nights to keep me awake. I have money in the bank for the first time in my life. Whereupon I discover that all that time I wasn't discriminated against like I thought. I was just broke, and up to my elbows in unpaid bills and kids screaming and nylons and diapers hanging in the bathroom. So now"—he flapped a hand—"so now, at age forty-six—a detective lieutenant with a locked-in pension—I discover that, by God, I'm being discriminated against. For being overweight." He pointed to the memo, looked at me reproachfully, and then uttered the single word "jogging" as if it were an obscenity.

3

I moved the memo aside, searching for a particular lab report analyzing the contents of a suspect's ashtray, large amber glass, File H-1843-B, Exhibit 7. My eyes burned and my arms felt heavy. There'd been two homicides in San Francisco the previous night. A hooker had been found knifed and robbed at about nine P.M.; a housewife had been found bludgeoned and robbed approximately four hours later. I'd just gotten the first investigation organized when the second call had come over the air. I'd gotten home at four A.M. I was up at eight A.M.; by nine A.M. I was dozing in a courtroom antechamber, waiting to testify in a fatal child-beating case. Now, at three P.M., I intended to empty my *In* basket, then go home.

"My informants tell me," Friedman was saying, "that you and the captain are in collusion on this—this jogging thing."

"Not true. He asked me what I thought about the idea. I said that it sounded fine."

"There is nothing," he said with solemn emphasis, "in either the California Civil Service Code or the San Francisco Police Department Manual that can get me jogging twice a week. Nothing at all."

I shrugged, paper-clipping a sheaf of onionskin interrogation transcripts, still searching for the missing lab report. Finally I dropped the transcripts into my top desk drawer, along with the contents of my *In* basket. I slid the drawer shut and got my gun from another drawer, locking the desk. Then, yawning and leaning back in my chair, I smiled faintly as I clipped on the gun. Friedman's bullfrog eyes were regarding me with an expression of betrayed accusation.

"You want the truth?" I asked.

He nodded.

"Well, the truth is, a couple of weeks ago I was having lunch with the captain. In the cafeteria. And it just so happened that both you and Canelli came in at the same time, and started loading up your trays. Now, you'll have to admit that the sight of you and Canelli together, in profile, loading up on calories, was a lot for the captain to take. He's supposed to be commanding a division of hard-bitten detectives. So when he looks up, halfway through his soup, and sees—"

4

"All right." He held up a beefy hand. "I've heard enough. I'll handle it myself."

"How?"

"Never mind. Are you going off duty?"

"Yes."

He leaned laboriously forward in his chair, retrieved the memo, then sank back with a sigh. "When the captain hand-delivered this to me," Friedman said, "he told me to take over the Moresco case from you, on the theory that two cases in one night is too much for one man, even if he does have a thirty-four-inch waist. I suppose," he added heavily, "that Moresco is the hooker. Right?"

"Right."

"Who's got the file?"

With difficulty, I kept my face straight. "Canelli had it this morning, as a matter of fact. He's out in the field, so the file is probably back in Records."

He studied me for a long, sardonic moment before saying, "What you're telling me, then, is that Canelli is on the case."

"Count your blessings. Canelli is the luckiest man in the history of the Inspectors' Bureau. You've said so yourself. Not the smartest. Not the most ambitious, or the slimmest. But the luckiest."

"Well, next time you see Captain Kreiger, reporting on the progress of your devious little jogging scheme, no doubt, you can say that Canelli and I will—"

My phone rang.

"Lieutenant Hastings," I answered, watching Friedman extract a cigar from an inside pocket, then heave himself laboriously from side to side, grunting and frowning as he rummaged for a match.

"Anything look promising on those two new ones, Frank?" It was Kreiger's voice: crisp, neutral, controlled. As always.

"Not much, I'm afraid."

"I promised the reporters I'd meet with them in a couple of hours—five o'clock. If you get anything new, be sure and give it to me."

"Right."

5

"Have you given Pete the Moresco case?"

"Yes."

"Is he there with you?"

"Yes."

"Tell him what I told you, then. About the news conference."

"Yessir." I hung up, eying Friedman as he lolled belly-up in my visitor's chair, puffing on the cigar and absently brushing at his ash-spotted vest.

"I'd offer you a cigar," he said, "but it'd be bad for your wind."

I glanced at the clock, then took ten minutes to outline the Moresco case, finishing with the admonition that the captain wanted something newsworthy by five P.M.

Friedman grunted. "The captain has one failing. He expects us to write his press-conference material for him."

I thought about it, then slowly nodded.

"He's also been saying too much to the reporters lately. One of these days he's going to get himself socked with a libel suit. Whereupon he'll lose his clear shot at the deputy chief's job." Friedman aimed the soggy end of his cigar at me, his shrewd, narrowed eyes suddenly serious. "You should tell him, Frank. You're old football buddies—army buddies. You should buy him a drink and pick the right time and tell him to let the reporters work a little harder. Christ, Kreiger's usually about as talkative as a cowboy sucking on a straw, and until just recently he was the same way with the press. Now, though—the past few weeks—when those reporters start working on him, he sings like a stoolie raising muscatel money."

"He'd agree with you," I said shortly. "I've already mentioned it."

"What's he say?"

"He says that the chief wants it this way. Public relations. Part of the new departmental image."

He grimaced. "And the chief, no doubt, has been talking to our brand-new mayor-elect. Mr. Public Relations himself."

I shrugged, abruptly dropping a paperweight on a stack of miscellaneous unclassified documents and letters.

"You're not going off duty after all," Friedman said, examining his cigar's precarious ash. "You're going to tough it out—dig up a news item. With three hours' sleep."

"I'm going to tough it out until five o'clock. Just like you are."

"How's your case look?"

"Not as good as yours. All you've got to do is find the Moresco girl's pimp, and you'll come up a hero."

"You don't have any leads on that housewife thing, eh?"

"Not yet."

"What was her name, anyhow?"

"Draper. Susan Draper." I got to my feet. "Which is where I'm going: the Draper house. Are you going to sit there and smoke, or do you want to walk down to the elevator?"

Not bothering to reply, Friedman heaved himself to his feet and followed me out of the office, trailing cigar ashes.

2

I pulled to a stop, set the brake, then checked my watch. The time was 3:50 P.M. I had exactly an hour in which to concoct a news item for the captain's news conference.

I sat behind the wheel for a moment, surveying the scene of the Draper murder: a narrow one-story stucco row house, one of thousands built during the late thirties and early forties. I'd lived my first seventeen years in San Francisco. I could remember watching those row houses slowly, inexorably propagating themselves like long, segmented worms, finally covering the wide, rolling sand dunes, my own private wonderland. As a small child, I'd chased howling, warpainted Indians across those dunes. As a teenager, parked on a freshly paved, sand-dusted street, surrounded by the bare nighttime skeletons of half-finished houses, I'd first touched the warm, secret flesh of Jacqueline Grant. We'd been fifteen. Earlier in the day—a Sunday —I'd first seen my name in print. As a sophomore fullback, I'd made the varsity squad, second string. Derek Rawlings had come by for me in his wheezing, chugging Model A. Both wearing our letter sweaters—mine two days old—we'd picked up Derek's girl friend, then Jacqueline. The four of us had spent the long, sunny Sunday together, riding in the Model A, sprawling on the beach, chasing each other, prancing through the surf. Later, as we awkwardly, ardently strained together in the anonymous darkness of the car's rear seat, I'd been conscious of the smell of salt water and sweat and the urgent musk of love—Jacqueline's and mine, mingled.

I sighed, blinking my eyes against the burning of last night's fatigue—and against the unexpected sharpness of sensations remembered almost thirty years later.

She'd be forty-three now. My age.

I got out of the cruiser, locking the door. I'd parked across the street from the Draper house, and I stood for a moment surveying the scene. Daylight made a difference. Daylight, and the muted shouts of playing children, and the endless row of look-alike houses, each of them built on a twenty-five-foot lot, a hundred feet deep, each with precisely three inches of air space separating it from its neighbor, according to the city code. Most of the houses were fussily well kept, with elaborate drapery at the front windows. The Draper house, though, didn't quite match up. The small front lawn was pale green, splotched with brown. The border plantings were only half tended. A small pane of glass in the garage door was broken.

A patrol car was parked directly in front of the house, a patrolman slumped behind the wheel. When he recognized me, he sat up abruptly. He was a young, lean, serious-looking cop, and I saw him swallowing as he half saluted, tentatively smiling.

"Hello, Lieutenant."

"Hi. Anything doing?"

"Nothing, Lieutenant. They haven't left the house, either the husband or the little girl. Haven't peeped out, either. Not since I came on, anyhow."

"When was that?"

"One P.M."

"Anyone try to get inside?"

"A couple of reporters and one neighbor. A few kids, too, and a paperboy. None of them gave me any trouble, though."

"Did the neighbor look all right?"

"As far as I could see—just a woman. I mean—" He cleared his throat, glancing sideways at me, then shrugging uncertainly. "I mean, she was a little fat, wearing a housedress and run-over shoes. And she went back to her house, three doors down, there. So—"

Again he shrugged, raising his hand from the steering wheel, gesturing down the block.

I nodded. "Okay. Good. Where's Inspector Markham?"

He pointed across the street, indicating a pink stucco house trimmed in gleaming white. "Inspector Markham's been over there for about forty-five minutes or so. Inspector Sigler went down to the Welfare Department, where the victim works. Worked, I mean."

I nodded again. "Tell Inspector Markham I'm going to talk to Mr. Draper. Do you happen to know the little girl's name—the victim's daughter?"

"Gee, I don't, Lieutenant. Sorry."

"That's all right. Is the back covered?"

"Yessir. My partner's back there. I mean, he's actually in the basement, where he can see the back door."

"Okay. See you in a few minutes."

I walked around the car, heading for the Drapers' front door. As I walked, I was recalling the details of last night's preliminary investigation: She'd apparently been an ordinary, average housewife, age thirty-two, comfortably married, a working mother. Name, Susan Draper. Medium build, medium features. Brunette. She'd gone out about eight-thirty P.M., heading for a Sunday night movie, leaving her husband home to mind the only child, a daughter. The husband put the daughter to bed at about nine, then watched TV until approximately midnight, when he retired. He read for a few minutes, then slipped off to sleep, still with the bedroom light on. He awoke at approximately 1:15 A.M. He didn't know whether anything had awakened him, or whether he'd just opened his eyes. His wife wasn't there. He decided to check on her, and went to the garage, using an inside stairway to the ground-level basement-garage, which extended the full width and length of the house. He discovered that he'd neglected to unbolt the inside access door to the garage, so that his wife had to enter the house by the front door, passing through the narrow, thickly planted tunnel entrance, then climbing the outside stairs to the front door.

Entering the garage, Mr. Draper found the car parked, the overhead garage door closed and locked. He'd slid the door up and left it open, intending to reenter the house as he'd left it, locking up behind. He'd walked to his right a few paces, then turned into the tunnel entrance leading up to the front door. The entrance was planted with large, broad-leafed plants, growing thickly. Mr. Draper had immediately seen his wife's feet protruding from the shrubbery. She'd been lying on her back, eyes open, staring straight up. Her purse had been torn from her arm, its strap broken. The wallet from the purse had been taken; the purse had been discarded at the scene. Mrs. Draper had been hit repeatedly on the head, probably with an iron pipe. Her husband had phoned Taraval Station a little after one-thirty.

Now, standing in the tunnel entrance, I saw the six-inch bloodstain on the sidewalk and the brown spatterings on the nearby foliage. According to the coroner, she'd probably been hit first on the right side of the skull as she was preparing to ascend the first step leading up to the front door. Her assailant, then, had been hiding in the shrubbery, waiting—the familiar mugger's M.O.

Except that muggings, statistically, seldom end in murder.

Perhaps she'd struggled, or cried out. Perhaps he'd hit her first to quiet her down—then lost control of himself. Either way, considering the close quarters of the entryway, the murderer must have spattered himself with blood.

I knelt down to examine the planting area's soft earth, now completely reproduced in interlocking plaster casts. Markham's preliminary report indicated that Mr. Draper's footprints had probably obliterated any meaningful evidence.

As I climbed the stairs my legs were heavy, my feet lagged. With three hours' sleep, I owed myself an evening in pajamas, watching an hour of TV, then going to bed for ten hours.

Mr. Draper answered the door on my second ring. He was a stocky man of medium height, dressed in slippers, casual slacks and a pullover fisherman's sweater. He was probably in his middle thirties, with blond hair thinning in front, worn long over his ears and thick at the back of his neck. He was a handsome, restless-looking man. His eyes were brown and wide-set. His mouth was wide and firm, but somehow too perfect: an actor's mouth. His manner, I'd decided last night, was petty and self-indulgent. He probably had a quick, unpredictable temper and an inflated idea of his own importance—a vain, hollow man, essentially weak. Last night he'd done little more than stare down at his toes, slowly shaking his head, constantly mumbling that he must be dreaming.

Now he was frowning at me, as if he was trying to focus his eyes. He seemed puzzled, vague—in delayed shock. He didn't recognize me.

I took off my hat, then introduced myself, apologizing for the intrusion. Still, I said, there were questions that must be asked, the sooner the better.

Sighing deeply, raggedly, he abruptly turned away, walking into the living room, leaving me to close the front door. He slumped down on a sofa, gesturing me to a facing chair. Shakily he took a cigarette from a crumpled pack lying on the cluttered, glass-ringed coffee table.

"I'll be as brief as I can, Mr. Draper," I began. "Last night—this morning, really—you weren't up to answering any questions for us. And for that matter, we weren't really sure what we needed to ask. Now, though, if you're willing, I'd like to ask you a few things."

As I'd been talking, he'd stared fixedly into my eyes, but I had the impression that he wasn't really listening. Now, as soon as I stopped speaking, his head dropped, as if it had been held erect by my words alone.

"Have you found him yet?" he mumbled, sucking on the cigarette. "Have you found out who did it?"

"Not yet, Mr. Draper."

"Do you think you will?"

"I can't really answer that, except to say that it may depend on how much you can help us."

He raised his head slowly, meeting my eyes. The process seemed to require great effort.

"How can I help?" As he said it, his handsome face seemed to be shrinking on itself. The eyes were suddenly more prominent; the actor's mouth distended. For a moment I thought of Dorian Grey: instant, incredible aging.

12

"Inspector Markham showed you her purse, didn't he?" I asked quietly.

He nodded.

"Was anything missing—anything but the wallet?"

"Not—" He cleared his throat. "Not that I could see. Is—is that important?"

"It could be important. A lot of these crimes, you see, are committed by narcotics addicts—people desperate for money. They steal whatever they can find, and turn it into money, usually by pawning whatever they steal. So if your wife had a valuable ring, for instance, that had been stolen, it might've been a lead for us, because it could turn up in a pawnshop."

"Yes. I—I see."

"But you can't recall anything that was missing," I pressed.

"No. Nothing."

"Have you given Inspector Markham a complete list of her credit cards and charge-a-plate accounts?"

"Yes."

"Good." I allowed a moment to pass, then said, "Her wristwatch, I noticed, was still on her wrist."

Not replying, he abruptly stubbed out his cigarette in the overflowing ashtray, then sat staring sightlessly down at the floor. His hands, resting on his knees, were clenched knuckle-white.

"The way she was lying," I said slowly, "the wristwatch was in plain view. I especially noticed it last night, because the angle of light from the street lamp in front of your house made the watch very obvious."

His only reaction was to catch his breath sharply, then slowly exhale in a long, ragged sigh.

"Did your wife have any enemies, Mr. Draper?"

He slowly, doggedly shook his head. His hands were still tightly clenched.

"Answer me, please," I said quietly. "I know it's a tough time for you. But we need answers. And time may be important."

Still shaking his head, he said indistinctly, "No. No enemies."

"Your wife worked at the Welfare Department, I understand."

"Y—yes."

"Was she a social worker?"

He nodded.

"And where do you work, Mr. Draper?"

"I'm a photographer."

"Are you employed by anyone?"

"No. I—I'm self-employed."

"Do you work out of your home?"

"Yes."

"What kind of photography do you do?"

He unclenched one fist, vaguely waving a soft, pale hand. "Anything I can get. Portraits, advertising shots. Anything."

"Are you reasonably successful, would you say?"

As if puzzled, he frowned petulantly. "Wh—what's that got to do with it—whether I'm successful or not?"

"It's what we call background information, Mr. Draper. We try to find out everything about a victim—everything about his life, his family situation, his work. Sometimes, when we add it all up, we get a picture that means something."

"But—" His puckered, perplexed face now seemed to reflect an almost childlike disappointment. "But you should be out trying to—to find the man. The one who killed her."

Ignoring the remark, I sat looking at him steadily, until he finally dropped his eyes. Then, deliberately, I asked, "Were you and your wife on good terms, Mr. Draper?"

Slowly, wonderingly, he raised his eyes, frowning and blinking, as if he couldn't comprehend. Then the muscles of his face began to bunch together in a twitching imitation of righteous, outraged anger.

"Of course we were on good terms." He hesitated, then: "We —we were married. For ten years."

I suppressed a smile. As a motive for murder, marriage topped the list. I said, "You *were* on good terms with your wife, then. You never fought."

"Well—" He hesitated. "I wouldn't say that, exactly. But we—"

"What about yesterday, Mr. Draper? Was it a usual day? A normal Sunday?"

For a moment he simply looked at me as if he hadn't heard. Then, allowing his head to sink, he mumbled, "Perfectly normal."

"Did you stay home all day? The family, I mean."

"Yes. It—it was raining. Besides, we were wrapping Christmas presents. Susan—my wife—wanted to get some presents off today. To her folks, in St. Louis."

"So nothing unusual happened yesterday? Is that right?"

"Yes."

"And nobody left the house until about eight-thirty, when your wife went to the movies."

He nodded.

"I was wondering," I said slowly, "why your wife went to the movies alone."

"To save on baby-sitting," he said dully. "We took turns."

I nodded, studying him silently—until he again dropped his eyes, fumbling for another cigarette. Then I reached for my hat, perched on a corner of the coffee table.

"Well," I said, "I'll be on my way. If we discover anything, we'll be sure and let you know. I suppose you're going to be here in the house."

"Yes, I—I guess so. I—I really can't—" He didn't finish it, shakily lighting the cigarette.

I fingered the crease in my hat, watching him as he sucked ravenously at the cigarette, drawing a glowing quarter-inch, deeply exhaling. Then, taking the cigarette from his mouth, he studied the burning end intently, oblivious to me. I saw him begin to swallow rapidly, at the same time blinking and frowning, his face and forehead glistening with sweat.

"If I hadn't bolted that door when she left," he said indistinctly, still staring at the cigarette, "she'd be alive right now. It was my fault—all my fault."

I looked at him a moment, then rose to my feet. "Everyone makes mistakes, Mr. Draper. Everyone in the world. I'll be going now. We'll be in touch with you whenever we find out anything."

He nodded loosely, then shook his head, and slowly, mechanically, raised the cigarette up to his mouth, as if the process required all his concentration and most of his strength.

I let myself out, closing the door softly behind me. As I was descending the front steps, I remembered that I'd forgotten to ask about the little girl, whose name I still didn't know.

3

Markham was sitting in the back seat of my car, listening to the radio. I slid into the front seat, twisting to face him.

"Anything?" I asked, nodding to the radio as I turned down the volume.

"No."

I glanced at my watch: 4:25 P.M. Twenty minutes, and I'd have to find a phone, report to Kreiger. I put my hat on the seat beside me, then slowly massaged my closed eyes with thumb and forefinger. Markham, I knew, hadn't had any more sleep than I'd had. But at twenty-eight he looked alert and clear-eyed, on top of the job. Which was another reason, I thought wryly, for not liking Markham. That, and his cold, vicious temper. He'd been on report twice during the past three years for using unnecessary force subduing suspects in custody. Both the suspects had been black. One had gone to the hospital with a ruptured spleen. The other eventually died.

I'd only once seen Markham hit a man, but I'd never forgotten it. He'd coolly watched for an opening, then stepped in close, dropped one shoulder, and hit the suspect just below the heart. The blow traveled only a few inches, but the suspect had dropped in his tracks. I'd been standing so that I could see Markham's eyes: killer's eyes, expressionless, except for an almost imperceptible glint of pleasure.

Still, Markham was an intelligent, hard-working, conscientious cop. He could think on his feet, and he wasn't afraid. He was cautious, but willing to gamble in the crunch. His sadistic temper had never distorted his judgment. And he was ambitious; he'd already passed his sergeant's exam, and was rising on the list. When Kreiger made Chief of Detectives, and Friedman made Captain, Markham would probably be my co-lieutenant. I didn't like the idea, but I couldn't think of a more qualified man.

"How's it look?" I asked, gesturing toward the Draper house.

Markham took a moment to adjust his tie, then said, "According to the background information, the Drapers didn't get along. He's too lazy to make much of a living, and she didn't let him forget it. About half the time he's minding the kid while she works—worked. One neighbor, apparently the local gossip, said that Mrs. Draper's father sends them checks all the time—even made a big down payment on their house. All of which bugs Draper, especially when he's drinking, which seems to be a lot of the time. Anyhow, the basement is filled with empty bottles. According to my informant, Mrs. Draper refused to throw out their empty liquor bottles because she didn't want to make a bad impression on the garbage man."

"What did Draper tell you about his movements yesterday?"

Markham eyed me for a moment, thoughtfully scrubbing his heavy five-o'clock stubble. "I thought you were just talking to him."

"I was." I said it quietly.

"Well," he answered reluctantly, "Draper says it was just an ordinary day. But their next-door neighbor—the gossip—says that she heard them arguing from about seven o'clock until Mrs. Draper went to the movies. No one else seems to've heard it, though."

"Did you talk to the little girl?"

His glance slid aside. "No. Not yet," he answered shortly. "I was going to do that next."

"Does it look like a regular mugging to you?"

He eyed me cautiously, alert for a trap. "It looks more like a mugging than a husband-and-wife thing. Draper might not be any prize, but he's no Yo-Yo, either. He's smart. And murdering your wife in the front entryway with an iron pipe isn't very smart. Not compared to pushing her down a flight of inside stairs, for instance, then finishing her off."

"Where was he when the uniformed men arrived?"

"In his daughter's room, checking on her."

"How long did it take the uniformed men to answer the call?"

"I'm not sure," he answered reluctantly. Then, defensively: "We haven't checked everything out yet. I haven't even been able to make a decent search for the weapon. There's just Sigler and me, you know."

I nodded, deciding not to make the elapsed time of the radio car's response an issue. Markham would find out before I saw him to-morrow. If I didn't press him, he'd volunteer the information, off-handedly. Markham resented direct orders.

I glanced at my watch. Ten minutes, and I'd have to leave, still without anything new for Kreiger. Irrelevantly, I was remembering the moment when I'd waited for my cue during the high school sen-ior play. It was a moment that could still come back in uneasy dreams.

"How about witnesses?" I asked.

He moved his head toward the pink-and-white house directly across from the Draper place. "The only thing I've been able to turn up is over there: a sixteen-year-old girl named Cindy Wallace. Last night she and her boyfriend were parked about where we're parked now, from approximately eleven-thirty till one. I couldn't get her away from her mother, but I get the impression that Cindy and her boyfriend were necking. I also figured out, from the way the car was parked, that the boyfriend would've been facing the Draper house, assuming they really were necking. Which, as a matter of fact, they might not've been really doing. At least, not all the time."

"How do you mean?"

"I got the impression that they might've had an argument. Any-how, she let it slip that she went into the house by herself. Then she let it slip that her boyfriend stayed parked in front of the house for ten or fifteen minutes after she went inside. I figured he might've been sitting in the car steaming at her."

"Who's her boyfriend?"

He'd anticipated the question, sliding his notebook smoothly from his pocket. Everything Markham did seemed smooth, effortless, self-contained. "Here it is," he said. "Dan Haywood. He lives at seventeen sixty-one Greenwich."

"That's just a couple of blocks from my place," I said, surprised. "Just around the corner, I think."

Not commenting, he slid the notebook back into his pocket.

"Do you think he might have something for us?" I glanced at my watch.

Markham shrugged. "Maybe. I thought I'd go over there later."

"I've got to phone the captain," I said. "I'll tell you what: I'll talk to this Dan Haywood on my way home. If I get anything important, I'll get back to you through Communications. Otherwise, I'll see you in the morning. In the meantime," I said, "maybe you should question Draper again. I can't tell whether he's in shock or worried stiff. But the book says the husband is suspect number one. And the book is usually right. So if you think you want to get a search warrant, go ahead."

He nodded in grudging agreement, leaving the car without looking back. As I watched him move smoothly, self-confidently across the street, I was thinking that he moved like a stereotyped Western badman, stalking his prey down a dusty, deserted street.

I was also thinking that because I'd suggested it, he would delay getting the search warrant, hopeful of breaking the case on his own terms.

4

I'd been right about 1761 Greenwich; the address was one of a pair of sizable flats, a block and a half from my apartment.

As I pressed the buzzer, I glanced around the neat, well-maintained premises, then noted the expensive wooden shutters in the Haywoods' lower flat. Rent, I calculated, between two-fifty and three hundred. Husband and wife probably college-educated, kids probably overprivileged. Not much to worry about; not much contact with the police, if you didn't count traffic tickets.

On the second ring, I heard footsteps approaching. As the door opened, I checked the time: 5:15 P.M. Kreiger was fifteen minutes into his news conference, faking it.

A tall, good-looking teenager stood in the doorway—a blond boy with a five-dollar razor cut, wearing an expensive wool sweater, wrinkled khaki slacks and stained, run-over tennis shoes. He held himself with the casual, offhand arrogance of the surfer—a young, golden beach god, accustomed to admiring stares.

I identified myself, verifying that the boy's name was Dan Haywood.

"Are your parents in?" I asked.

"No," he answered shortly. He was standing squarely in the doorway, one hand braced against the frame. His eyes were calm and steady, unrevealing.

"When do you expect your parents?"

He shrugged. "My mother's downtown shopping. My father—won't be in."

I nodded, shifting my weight as I took a long, silent moment to look him up and down, deliberately.

"What's it all about, anyhow?" he asked.

Pausing another deliberate moment, I decided on a casual tone as I said, "I'm checking out a statement that we received from Miss Cindy Wallace, concerning her movements last night. She said she was with you from approximately eleven-thirty until one. Is that right?"

"Did you say you're a lieutenant?"

"That's right."

He nodded, pressing his lips together in an expression of cool, show-me speculation. "That's pretty high up, just to be checking on what old Cindy was doing last night. I mean, you can't be after her for anything very heavy."

I drew a deep, weary breath, recognizing the beginning of an old, familiar routine: the games that tough, street-wise teenagers play, impressing each other.

"How old are you, Dan?" I asked quietly. "Sixteen?"

He nodded. His eyes, almost level with mine, were watchful. His wide, well-shaped mouth mocked me faintly.

"Last night was Sunday," I said. "Why were you out so late on a Sunday?"

He smiled, enjoying our little game. "This is the first day of Christmas vacation, Lieutenant."

I looked at him, not saying a word, until he began to shift uncomfortably, finally dropping his eyes. Then I asked casually, "What've you been doing all day, Dan?"

He shrugged loosely, allowing his head to sag to one side. The mannerism, I saw, was a habit. "A bunch of us took off down the Skyline, hitting the beaches."

"Isn't it a little cold to be hitting the beaches?"

He smiled smugly. "We keep warm."

"What time did you leave this morning?"

"Just before noon. We got back a couple of minutes before you came. They just dropped me off."

"You didn't talk to Cindy today, then."

"No."

"Did you hear any news reports today—see any papers?"

His eyes widened. I recognized that expression, too: the uncertain child peeking from behind a mask of worldly teenage cynicism.

"Hey—" His voice slipped higher. "Are you telling me that"— he swallowed, involuntarily stepping back—"that something's happened to Cindy?"

"No, Dan. I'm just saying that—" I saw his eyes dart over my shoulder. Turning, I saw a small, good-looking woman standing on the sidewalk a few paces behind me. She was tentatively, inquiringly smiling. She wore boots, a heavy wool skirt and a short leather jacket. Her hair was a thick, tawny blond, tied with a bright paisley scarf. Her eyes were gray, her manner calm and appraising. She was carrying three sizable packages, Christmas-wrapped.

"This is my mother," the boy said defensively.

I touched my hat, identifying myself—watching her quick eyes dart apprehensively to her son, then back to me. With open reluctance she preceded me into the comfortably furnished living room. We sat facing each other across a small marble coffee table. The boy lounged slouching in the doorway, pantomiming street-corner insolence.

"Why don't you sit down, Dan?" I gestured to a nearby chair. Shrugging, he sat down, sighing deeply.

Turning to Mrs. Haywood, I told her sketchily about the Draper murder, and about Cindy Wallace's statement concerning her son. As I talked, I watched her expression change from frowning, finger-twisting foreboding to quick, eye-widened alarm at the mention of murder. Finally, as I concluded, she seemed plainly relieved, relaxing back into her chair, unclasping her fingers. Yet, somehow, the gestures calculated to signify relief seemed subtly forced. Her eyes seemed too bright, her posture too ostentatiously at ease.

"So what I want from your son," I said finally, "is a clear statement of everything he did last night, between the time he parked across from the Draper home until the time he returned here." As I said it, I turned to Dan expectantly.

"Tell him, Dan." Her voice was low, her eyes shadowed, uncertain. In that moment I realized that she was unable to control her son. I also realized that she was divorced. She was doing her best, but failing. Every policeman constantly encounters that same shadow of despairing doubt deep in the eyes of an unhappy woman.

Looking expressionlessly at his mother, the boy seemed to study her with disdainful disapproval. Then, turning to me, he said, "You've got it right—just like old Cindy said. We got there about eleven-thirty. I guess I probably left about twelve-thirty. Maybe a little later." He smiled sardonically. "I wasn't checking the time."

For a moment I didn't reply. Suddenly I wondered whether it could have been this boy who had bludgeoned Mrs. Draper to death.

Could he have flipped because Cindy Wallace wouldn't put out for him? Had he then seen Mrs. Draper emerging from her garage, and focused his frustration on her? Teenagers, over the sexual edge, were incredibly unpredictable. Plainly, Dan Haywood was a defensive, spoiled, basically unhappy kid, loaded with enough hostility to trigger violence.

"While you were parked," I asked, "did you see Mrs. Draper drive into her garage?"

He shook his head, then shifted abruptly in the chair, slipping farther down on his spine as he crossed one khaki leg over the other, ankle-to-thigh. He began twitching the dangling foot.

"Answer me, Dan," I said quietly. "Don't just shake your head."

"All right," he said. "Then no." His voice was edged with a plaintive whine.

"You didn't see her."

"Right." He bobbed his head loosely. "I didn't see her."

"Did you see anyone on the Draper premises? Any movement in the shrubbery, for instance?"

"No, nothing. I—" He frowned, then sat up straighter. "Hey—maybe I did, at that."

I allowed a moment to pass, wondering why he'd changed his mind.

"You saw something, then."

"Well—" He spread his hands. "I *guess* I did. I mean, people were walking by, you know, all the time. But now that I think about it, I did see this black guy kind of loitering around across the street."

"In front of the Drapers', you mean?"

"Around there. Yeah."

"Did you get a good look at him?"

"No. I remember that he was tall, though. Tall and skinny." I looked at him. "As tall as you are, for instance?"

Cautiously he met my glance, then frowned, looking away. "About as tall as I am, I guess."

Then I asked, "Did you take Cindy Wallace to her door when you said goodnight, Dan?"

For a long moment he didn't reply. Then, slowly, he said, "No. She—she went in by herself."

I nodded, deciding not to press the point. I'd let him wonder for a while how much I knew about their quarrel.

"So then you came home," I said.

"Yes."

"Directly home?"

"Sure, directly home." He looked at his mother, smirking faintly. "In bed by one."

I pretended to think about it while I watched him shift in his chair, twitching his foot and gnawing at his lips. Plainly, now, something was bothering him. Did it concern Cindy Wallace or Susan Draper? Or both?

It was time to ease off—give him some slack.

Leaning forward in my chair, I decided to smile at the boy. "I guess that'll be all for now, Dan. I'll give my card to your mother. If you remember anything else, especially concerning the black man you saw, be sure and call me."

He immediately got to his feet. He nodded to me once, jerkily, then left the room, ignoring his mother.

I sighed, searched in my pocket, and laid a business card on the small marble table. Then I raised my eyes to find the mother watching me, blinking rapidly.

"What's it all about, Lieutenant?" Her voice was tight and low. "What's it really all about?"

I decided to say, "I'm not keeping anything from you, Mrs. Haywood. It's possible that your son could've seen Mrs. Draper's murderer. If so, Dan's an important witness."

"The black man, you mean."

"Hmm."

She was sitting in what my wife used to call a "finishing-school posture"—feet flat on the floor, knees pressed primly together, hands gracefully clasped and resting on the knees. Mrs. Haywood, obviously, had class. Just as obviously, she had something on her mind.

Did she suspect that her son could have murdered the Draper woman?

Had she found his bloodstained clothing?

Had she found the weapon, concealed?

I saw her glance surreptitiously at her watch. It was 5:45, probably she had to prepare dinner. But my business there was unfinished.

"Do you have just the one child, Mrs. Haywood?"

She abruptly shook her head, as if the question required a quick denial. "No. I have a younger son. Age ten."

"Two children."

"Yes."

I paused, thought about it, then asked, "Were you and your husband home last night? Between, say, eleven and one?"

She lifted her chin, saying in a low voice, "I'm divorced, Lieutenant Hastings."

I nodded, smiling at her. "Same question, then. Different subject."

She answered my smile, said almost wistfully, "Yes. I was home all night."

"Were you still up when your son came home?"

"No. I went to bed about eleven-thirty."

Again I paused, then said, "Does your son often stay out after midnight, Mrs. Haywood?"

Still sitting in her finishing-school position, she was looking down at her gracefully clasped hands; after a moment she said, "The answer to that, I'm afraid, is yes."

"Did you know that Dan and Cindy Wallace were going out together last night?"

"Yes."

"What did they do during the early part of the evening?"

"They went to a movie."

"Do you know which movie?"

"I—I'm afraid not."

"Where does Dan go to school?"

"Galileo."

"Does he do well in his schoolwork?"

Very slowly, with obvious effort, she raised her head, meeting my eyes. Her chin was set firmly, but her wide gray eyes were painfully vulnerable. She drew a long, deep breath, raising her breasts taut beneath the leather jacket. She seemed to be in exhausted repose —a penitent drained by confession.

In that moment I felt myself stirred by her.

We were looking at each other, suspended together in a moment of questioning silence. Then, glancing away, she shook her head regretfully. "No, Lieutenant. Dan doesn't do well in his schoolwork. Which is doubly embarrassing, since I'm a teacher." She tried an unsuccessful smile.

I hesitated, then asked quietly, "Has Dan ever been in any trouble with the police, Mrs. Haywood?"

Once more looking down at her hands, she said, "Yes, he's been in trouble. About a year ago."

"What was the charge?"

"He and another boy got into a 'hassle,' as they call it, with a man on a streetcar. The man, apparently, was drunk, and the whole incident was terribly—unclear. But the two boys—Dan and his friend—spent the night in Juvenile Hall."

"What was the disposition of the case?"

"The usual: probation, discharged to parental custody. Actually—" She paused. "Actually, my ex-husband appeared in court. He's a psychoanalyst—a rather well-known psychoanalyst. He was very effective in court."

In recognition of her double defeat, I said, "Divorce is a messy business. I know."

She smiled wryly. "You're a member of the club, then."

"I'm afraid so. For nine years I've been a member."

Again she drew a deep breath. "That seems like a long time. It's been two years for me. And the second year seemed much, much longer than the first. At that rate of progression, I'll never make nine."

"It gets better with time. Or it aches less. Like everything else." I looked at her, hoping she'd meet my glance. When she didn't, I took my hat from the table. "Well, it's near your dinnertime." I rose. "I won't bother you any more right now. Your son isn't planning to leave town, is he?"

She'd risen with me; we were facing each other, a few feet apart. "He'll be here through Christmas. Then he and his brother are going skiing, with their father."

"Is their father remarried?"

She looked at me steadily. "Yes. He's been married for a year."

I nodded. "I know that feeling, too." I turned and walked out into the hallway, conscious that she was following close behind. At the door, I turned. "Does your son have his own car, Mrs. Haywood?"

"No. He uses mine."

"He was driving yours last night, then."

"Yes. He—"

A hallway door slammed; a small boy appeared, striding rapidly toward us. He was a slender, quick-moving boy with large, solemn eyes. He stood close to his mother, studying me intently. Then, abruptly, he asked, "Are you going to arrest my big brother?"

"No, I'm not."

He stepped away from his mother, standing spread-legged before me. He looked me up and down, ending his scrutiny at my hip. I knew he wanted to see my gun. He tilted his head up to look me squarely in the eye. "Good," he said. And, turning, he strode determinedly away. He looked like a miniature general inspecting the troops.

I watched him for a moment, then turned to the woman. "You're at least batting five hundred," I said. "Maybe more, eventually." Then, opening the door, I stepped out on the small stoop. A light December rain was beginning to fall. She switched on the porch light, then stood in the open doorway. With her arms folded, looking up at me, she seemed small and lonely.

"Thanks for your time, Mrs. Haywood. I'll be in touch with you. And don't worry." I saw her smile and nod. Then, moving my head toward the corner, I said, "We're neighbors. I didn't mention it, but I just live a block and a half from here."

Her small, wistful smile widened. "Good." She stepped back. "I'm glad." She hesitated, then added, "You won't get wet if you live that close."

Feeling strangely foolish, I tipped my hat, then turned away. As I walked to the car, I realized that the prospect of a quiet evening, early-to-bed, seemed suddenly less inviting.

5

The next morning, blearily waiting for the toast to pop, I grimaced to myself, recalling that I hadn't discovered Mrs. Haywood's given name. It was both a professional and a personal lapse. I couldn't properly enter "Mrs. Haywood" in a workmanlike interrogation report. And I couldn't properly conceive an erotic fantasy featuring a woman with no first name.

I was buttering the toast when the phone rang. Sighing, I lifted the receiver, automatically registering the time at 9:40.

"Lieutenant Hastings?"

"Yes."

"This is Canelli, Lieutenant."

"Hello, Canelli." Propping the phone on one shoulder, I reached for the blueberry jam. Canelli was constitutionally long-winded. "What's up?"

"Well, I was just writing up a report on that Moresco thing when we got a call on a double homicide, it sounds like. And the more I thought about it, considering that Lieutenant Friedman is out in the field and Captain Kreiger has an appointment for a physical, or something, the more I thought I should call you."

"Is Lieutenant Friedman still working on the Moresco case?"

"Yessir."

"How's it look?"

"Her pimp did it, nickels to dollar bills. It was the old story: she was turning tricks on the side. That's where Lieutenant Friedman is right now—him and Haskell are down at the pimp's lawyer's, or somewhere. He's one of those pimps with lots of money—Cadillacs, and silk suits, and everything. There's a D.A. guy there with them, so you know they're pretty close." He paused, then said, "Lieutenant Friedman told me to come down to the office, see, and do the paper work on Moresco. That's because I can touch-type."

"Hmm." As he'd been talking, I was biting into the toast. Now, chewing furtively, I asked, "What about this double homicide?"

"Well, that's why I'm calling. I mean, the call just came in from a radio car about two minutes ago. And the way it looks, this could be one of those with a lot of heat. It's in a fancy apartment in Pacific Heights, and everything, with maybe a lot of rich people involved. Plus it sounds kind of messy. So I thought you should know."

"Are any details available?"

"Two victims, a male and a female. Both dead from gunshot wounds. The cleaning lady discovered them about fifteen minutes ago, and fainted, then went into shock. That's all I know."

"How many prowl cars are on the scene?"

"Two. The lab guys are on the way. And I just notified the coroner."

"Who's in the office besides you?"

"Rawlings and Culligan. Markham and Sigler are coming down in about half an hour, but they're already working on something—that Draper case, I guess. Everyone else is out, except that a couple more are coming down before noon."

"All right, you and Culligan go on out to the Pacific Heights thing. What's the address?" Laying the toast aside, I reached for a pad of paper.

"It's twenty-seven thirty-one Jackson. Right near Scott."

"All right. You get things started, and I'll be along in twenty minutes. If you think you need more uniformed men, put in the call. When's the captain due on duty?"

"About eleven o'clock, according to Communications."

"I'll see you in twenty minutes or so. If you see Markham on your way out, tell him I'll be checking with him later on. Find out where he thinks he'll be after lunch."

"Yessir."

I pulled to a stop, checked out with Communications, then switched off the radio. For a moment I sat quietly behind the wheel, feeling comfortably anonymous—truant. During the last few blocks I'd been thinking of the Haywood woman, idly imagining situations in which I could make the transition with her from a policeman to simply a man. If I'd met her at a party, I could call her today, inviting her out for dinner. But as a policeman—a potential threat to her son —I could be her natural enemy. If she were attracted to me, it would seem to her an unnatural attraction—a perversion, almost.

In nine years I'd become accustomed to almost all the lonely little rites and rituals of a policeman's existence—the big and the little differences between myself and everyone else. I'd recognized, first, that the simple fact of a gun made the most significant difference: that cold, constant weight at the hip, on duty and off—forbidding the bearer certain small, insignificant freedoms: the right to wear sport shirts, or to romp spontaneously with children in the park, or to raise his arms too high when riding buses.

Next I'd learned the subtler facts of a policeman's life: the isolated, anonymous, inbred camaraderie compounded of the secret knowledge that brutality among cops is more common than kindness, and cowardliness more common than bravery. Finally—very, very slowly—I came to realize that the essential difference between a policeman and a civilian is the stark, simple fact that a cop, day after day and hour after hour, deals with the human animal at its worst. A policeman's stock in trade is human misery: robbery, rape, assault, murder. If someone isn't frightened or angry or bleeding or dead, there's no need for the police. A cop needs victims like a storekeeper needs customers: no victims, no job. And the job literally stinks, because the victims usually stink. If they're drunk or frightened, they vomit. If they're injured or dead, they void themselves.

So, slowly, a cop comes to realize that goodness and happiness and hope are merely happy human accidents that have nothing to do with him.

I drew a deep breath, and glanced up at the dark, overcast sky. Soon it would begin raining, and would continue, probably, all day.

I got out of the car and stood for a moment surveying the familiar scene: the cluster of curious onlookers, the official cars parked at odd, arrogant angles, the metallic voice of the police dispatcher droning monotonously through the muted sounds of the staid, affluent neighborhood.

The building at 2731 Jackson was typical of privileged San Francisco: two large, well-kept flats, probably forty years old, each with its separate entrance. In fact, it was similar to that in which the Haywoods lived. The rent, though, would be higher—easily twice as high, if the tenants had a view of the bay.

Sergeant Dave Pass, from Northern Station, stood at the door of the lower flat. Seeing me, he nodded, smiling and half-waving. Years ago, when I'd been a patrolman, we'd ridden together for a month or so. I'd been new on the job—an average rookie with too many memories. Pass had often covered for me, without comment or complaint.

As I strode up the short flagstone walkway, I glanced at the meticulously maintained shrubbery and the impeccably painted façade of the building. It was a completely restored Victorian, older than I'd thought and probably more expensive.

"Hello, Dave. How've you been?" I asked, shaking hands.

"Pretty good. I haven't seen you since you made Lieutenant. How's it seem?"

"The pay's better and the job isn't any harder, once you get used to letting someone else do the legwork." I moved my head toward the door. "What's it look like?"

He spread his hands. "Your boys are still inside, with the M.E. and the lab crew. I haven't heard a thing. I— Oh, oh." He moved his chin slightly toward the street. Following the gesture, I saw a *Sentinel* car pull to a stop. I opened the flat's front door, saying, "Tell them I'll have something for them in fifteen or twenty minutes. Have you got the back door covered?"

"Sure."

"Okay. See you later. Next time you're downtown I'll buy you a cup of coffee."

"I have to come down Friday. I'll take you up on it."

"Good." I stepped into the entryway, closing the door behind me just as the first reporter began plaintively arguing with Pass. Because of the dark day, the entry hall was dim. I switched on the lights, then stood perfectly still as I looked around, orienting myself.

The layout was typical of attached Victorian flats built on San Francisco's narrow twenty-five-foot lots. A long hallway stretched from the front door to the rearmost rooms, probably a spacious kitchen and a master bedroom. Off the single hallway the other rooms opened, one after the other.

Passing the living room, I casually looked inside. The room was incredibly disorganized—not ransacked, but simply jumbled together haphazardly. Taking the furniture item by item, the individual pieces were of superb quality, in excellent condition. Yet the room looked as if its last inhabitants had been destructive children playing house.

Stepping out into the hallway again, I saw Canelli waiting for me. Hands in his pockets, he was looking into the back room on the right. His suit was baggy and wrinkled. His shirt collar, mashed beneath massive jowls, was wilted and curled. His face, as usual, reflected a kind of preoccupied, faintly frowning perplexity. Canelli was twenty-eight, weighed two hundred forty pounds, and always needed a closer shave. He'd been engaged to a girl named Rosalie for six years. He was a good-natured, plodding, unimaginative cop whose greatest single virtue was a perpetual streak of incredible good luck in his job. Two weeks ago, standing in line waiting to deposit his paycheck at the Castro Branch of the Bank of America, Canelli had glanced over the shoulder of the man in front of him just as the man was passing a robbery note to the teller. Typically, in the brief struggle that followed, Canelli lost his paycheck, his bankbook and his wallet, none of which was recovered. Initialing the arrest report, Friedman had remarked that only Canelli could get robbed while he was arresting a robber.

Canelli's voice was hushed as he said, "Morning, Lieutenant."

"Good morning." I stood beside him, studying the murder scene.

He'd been right; it was a messy one.

A huge fourposter bed dominated the room. The ruffled canopy hung in shreds from one elaborately carved bedpost. The nude body of a man sagged against another post, suspended by his tied wrists like a crucified thief. He was of medium build, with dark hair worn long enough to almost cover his ears. His knees were bent, hanging less than a foot from the floor. From the lower abdomen down, his body was almost entirely covered with caked blood. Both shoulders had been dislocated by the weight of the hanging body. He was facing me, but his neck was bent, his features obscured.

The woman lay spread-eagled on the bed, face down. Her dark blond hair was almost waist-length. The hair was matted with blood in two small circular areas, one midway between the spine and the left shoulder, another in the exact center of the back. She was nude. On her right hand she wore a ring; on her left wrist, a wristwatch. She was average height, and probably weighed about a hundred thirty pounds. Her thighs were heavy; her toenails were painted red. No bloodstains were visible on the bedclothing beneath the body.

The room was crowded with hushed, carefully stepping men: a photographer, a fingerprint man, two lab technicians and the medical examiner, Roger Sobel. Two ambulance attendants stood against the wall, one of them holding a stretcher. The smell of double death was nauseating.

I inventoried the signs of a struggle: a chair was overturned, a lamp was smashed, cosmetics littered the floor. A large box of talcum powder had been spilled, dusting the thick gold rug. Someone had walked through the powder. Had it been the murderer? The maid?

"Where's Culligan?" I asked.

"Upstairs, talking to the neighbors."

I nodded, then stepped gingerly into the bedroom, walking between the lab's tape markers. I stood on a small bedside rug while I studied the man's corpse. His hands were tied with yanked-out telephone cord, wrapped a dozen times around the wrists, then crudely knotted. A crosspiece on the bed supported the body. The crosspiece was almost six feet from the floor. He'd been forced to stand beside the tall bedpost, then hold his hands in position while the murderer bound his wrists. The murderer might have stood on the bed while binding his victim.

Or, quite possibly, there'd been two murderers—a team.

He'd been shot twice in the abdomen. The wounds probably hadn't been fatal. Judging from the amount of blood, he'd probably bled to death.

Still standing in one spot, not touching the body, I knelt on one knee, staring up into the victim's face. He appeared to be in his early forties. His features were heavy and dark, but regular. His complexion was swarthy, his beard a heavy blue-black. His nose was a little too long for his face, his chin a little too small. His eyes were open, staring at my feet. His mouth gaped. On his right cheek was a fresh circular burn—a deep cigarette burn, deliberately inflicted. He'd been tortured.

I straightened, then turned to the woman's body. Her face was totally obscured, buried in the bedclothing. From the texture of her flesh, she seemed to be in her middle or late twenties. She'd been shot twice in the back. Beneath the distended swell of one flattened breast I saw the beginning of a huge bloodstain. She'd died where she'd fallen.

I nodded to Sobel, and told him that Canelli and I would wait in the kitchen, out of the way.

As we sat facing each other across a carved Mexican pedestal table, I glanced around the kitchen, assessing the expensive appliances, the walnut cabinets, the copper pots hung on an ornamental brick wall. The kitchen represented more money than I'd invested in my entire apartment. The sink and sideboard, predictably, were heaped with dirty dishes.

"Well," I said, "what've you got so far?"

"So far, not much," Canelli answered, flopping his notebook open on the table. "The cleaning lady, named Janice Henry, said that the victims are Karen Manley and Roberto Valenti. Whereupon she passed out. I sent her out to County Hospital."

"With a guard?"

"Well—" He cleared his throat.

"You'd better post a guard until we've talked to her. Just as soon as we've finished here."

"Yessir."

"Any sign of the weapon?"

"Not so far. But we haven't really checked. I mean, it isn't in the room."

"What else?"

He spread his hands. "Not much, I guess. I mean, Culligan's still upstairs talking to the neighbors. And I figured I should stay here to keep an eye on things. So—"

The back door opened. A moment later Culligan appeared in the doorway. He paused, grunted a greeting to me, then slumped abruptly into a chair. Culligan was Canelli's exact opposite: cadaverously thin, hollow-chested, balding, laconic and sour-tempered. His long, sad face was sallow and deeply lined, his small eyes seemed to be focused inwardly, his drawn mouth was permanently twisted into an expression of grim, long-suffering forbearance. Culligan was a worrier, with the ulcer to prove it. He was thirty-four but he looked fifty. His wife was a rangy, wide-hipped, slatternly woman whose eyes and mouth matched her husband's.

"This one," he said heavily, "is going to be a picnic for the newspapers."

"How's that?"

"Because the female victim, Karen Manley, is the daughter of Walter J. Manley, of Manley, Robbins and Quant. The stockbrokers. His family goes back to the gold rush. They own banks, office buildings—the works."

I snorted ruefully. As usual, Culligan wasn't exaggerating; if anything, he was understating the case. In San Francisco, the Manley name was synonymous with wealth, power and position. I glanced at my watch, wondering whether Kreiger could be reached.

"Who's the man?" I asked Culligan.

"His name is Roberto Valenti. According to the neighbors, he's a gigolo. No good."

"They weren't married, I take it."

"Not according to their neighbors. They moved into the apartment about six months ago. Since then they've done nothing but raise hell—all kinds of hell, all the time."

"How do you rate these neighbors as informants?"

Culligan thought about it, scowling as he gnawed at his lip. "I'd rate them about eighty percent," he said finally. "Good."

"What'd they say about last night?"

"According to them, it was just another ordinary night down here: people in and out at all hours, lots of noise, a couple of arguments. Nothing unusual."

"How about shots?"

"Well, Mr. Armstrong—the husband upstairs—said that he thought he heard shots at about two. He was asleep, but something woke him up. The shots, probably. However, he thought it was the TV, or something. Or the *1812 Overture*, whatever that is. Anyhow, he says he just rolled over and went back to sleep."

I nodded thoughtfully, for a long moment watching my own forefinger rhythmically tapping the wooden table. I was thinking that for the moment I'd have to forget about the Draper murder—and about Mrs. Haywood, the small, tense woman with the wide gray eyes and no first name.

I looked up to discover both men expectantly staring at me.

I turned first to Canelli. "You'd better get on the radio. Tell Communications to notify the captain. Then take care of that guard for the cleaning lady. Then get two more inspectors assigned to the case, on my authority. Tell them to report to me here, immediately. Then you start canvassing the neighbors for background information on the victims."

As Canelli left, I turned to Culligan. "Check with the lab team; see if you can use the phone here. Find either Mr. or Mrs. Manley. Make an appointment for me; tell them I'll be calling on them immediately. Don't tell them about the murder—just that there's been an accident. The usual." I paused, then added, "If there's a choice, I'll see the father, Mr. Manley. After you do that, get a couple of uniformed men and organize a search for the weapon." I paused, then added, "I'm putting you in charge."

Nodding, he tiredly unfolded himself, rising to his feet. Watching him shuffle out into the hallway, I wondered whether Culligan could have TB. Was he sick, or just unhappy? Or did the two ultimately go together?

I took out my notebook and headed a fresh page: Manley—Valenti. Then I began writing.

6

My first glimpse of Walter J. Manley evoked a vague sense of disembodied recall. As he rose to greet me, I recognized the wide, thick shoulders, the slightly bowed neck, the athlete's unmistakable air of muscular ease.

He'd played football in college—well-bred, overprivileged, very serious football. His beautifully barbered iron-gray good looks were typically the college athlete's after twenty-odd years of board-room triumphs.

I was prepared, then, for the whole weary scenario: first the firm, hard grip, then the slow glimmer of recognition as my name vaguely registered. And, finally, the up-and-down look of appraisal: the successful executive who'd never made the varsity, standing relaxed behind his desk and surveying the middle-aged ex-hero palming a worn leather billfold with silver shield attached.

His first question, though, concerned his daughter: "What's the trouble, Lieutenant?" He motioned me to a deep leather visitor's chair, then resumed his seat at the huge rosewood-and-chrome desk. His voice clearly revealed that he was a man used to taking charge in any interview.

Behind the rosewood desk, a glass-and-steel wall overlooked the city's most magnificent vista: the abstract shapes of skyscraper-slabs, the low, curving grace of the Bay Bridge, the dark green bulk of

Treasure Island, the slate-blue of the ship-dotted bay—all of it washed with a winter's blend of white fog-shreds and a brooding, monochromatic gray sky.

For a brief moment the view held me. Then, regretfully, I returned my gaze to the trim, handsome man in his vigorous middle fifties, looking at me now with intelligent, appraising eyes. He was on guard—politely, cautiously on guard. Getting down to business.

I told him that his daughter was dead.

Years of police work had taught me the value of observing first reactions. So I watched Manley's face intently as he blinked, exhaled and lowered his eyes. Then, slowly sinking back in his elegant chair, he seemed to absorb the shock in grimly controlled slow motion. His arms were extended, his palms flat on the rosewood desk, wide apart. He was staring at a spot precisely between his two widespread hands. The urbane, complacent contours of his face began to twitch. His face was pale beneath an expensive winter tan. He closed his eyes, set his jaw and slowly began shaking his head, eyes still closed.

Dispassionately assessing his reactions, I decided that Manley's responses were genuine, convincing.

He drew a long, shaky breath, then opened his eyes, still staring down at the desk. Finally, in a low, thick voice, he said, "I've been expecting it. For years I've been expecting it. Unconsciously, at least. What was it—drugs?"

Having decided that he probably possessed no guilty knowledge, and that he could take a second shock, I told him the details of Karen Manley's death. As I talked, watching his face, I saw the first pale, twitching tautness of despair change to flushed, eye-glittering outrage. As I finished talking, he began to swear—grimly, doggedly, obscenely.

"It's those goddamn degenerates," he said, finally coherent. "It's Valenti, and all the rest of them. They've—" He swallowed, setting his teeth, painfully bunching the muscles along his jaw. "They've ruined me. Ruined us. I should've—" He stopped suddenly.

"You should've what, Mr. Manley?" I asked quietly.

He slowly raised his eyes to glare at me, as if he just now fully realized the significance of my presence. He pushed himself up straighter in the chair, squared his shoulders, cleared his throat. Then, looking directly into my eyes, he said deliberately, "I should've killed him myself. That's what I was going to say, Lieutenant. Except that it wouldn't've done any good. Valenti was just a—a symptom, not a cause. He was just—" Suddenly he gulped, blinked, and shook his head. The spasm of outrage had passed; he'd sunk back into a wounded, hollow-eyed despair. "I'll have to tell my wife," he mumbled. He looked at me, woodenly polite, as he asked, "Do you know where she is, Lieutenant?"

"She's home, Mr. Manley."

He nodded. He lifted the phone and told someone, undoubtedly his secretary, to tell his wife that he'd be home in a half-hour. Then he ordered his car. Watching him give the orders, I glimpsed a pale shadow of the public Mr. Walter J. Manley: decisive, urbane, forceful—a prototypical member of the privileged class.

But as he placed the phone in its cradle a last time, his eyes again lost focus, as if the absence of actual physical contact with the telephone had deprived him of some necessary source of energy.

"Mr. Manley," I said, "I know you're anxious to see your wife. Understandably. But now I'd like you to take a few minutes and tell me anything that you think might help us find your daughter's murderer—anything at all. As you know, time is critical in police work. Right now—right this minute—your daughter's murderer is doing everything in his power to avoid detection. Maybe he's already on his way out of town. Or if he's still in San Francisco, he's going back over the crime, trying to remember every detail—looking for a mistake he might've made. If he remembers something he did wrong, he might be able to cover his tracks. Unless we get there first."

He was watching me intently, his gaze sharply, feverishly refocused. "Why do you say 'he'?" he asked. "Do you—know anything? Suspect anything?"

"No, Mr. Manley, we don't. It's just a figure of speech."

He nodded slowly. Then the brief, tense moment passed, leaving him strangely listless. Finally, with a kind of exhausted curiosity —as if compelled to escape momentarily the knowledge of his daughter's death—he asked, "Are you the same Frank Hastings who played football for Stanford, by any chance, and then went on to the Lions?"

"Yes, I am." I glanced pointedly at my watch.

"I thought so," he murmured. "I went to Stanford. Before you did." He looked at me for a final moment of exhausted appraisal, then dropped his eyes, sighing deeply. For a moment he seemed confused —drained. Then, shaking his head, he said, "She was only twenty-six, you know. She had her"—he gulped—"her whole life ahead of her."

I allowed a moment to pass, then asked him again for his statement. With visible effort he gathered himself together, then said, "Where do you want me to start, Lieutenant?"

"Start wherever you like, Mr. Manley. Maybe with your daughter's, ah, living habits—her known associates. Especially those who might've wanted to harm her."

"Or him." He pronounced the pronoun like an obscenity. "It's him, probably, that they were after. Not"—he swallowed—"not Karen."

"You might be right," I answered slowly. "Still, at this point, we need all the information we can get. Everything."

"Yes, of course." He nodded. Then, after a moment's painful thought, he said, "Karen met Valenti down in Los Angeles. It was about a year ago, I think. Maybe a little less."

"Was your daughter living in Los Angeles at the time?"

"Yes and no," he answered. "She lived there for some months, off and on. She wasn't settled there, though. But then, she wasn't settled anywhere. Not really."

"Give me a brief history of her life, Mr. Manley. A chronology. From, say, her late teens."

He began to blink, wonderingly. "Her late teens. That was less than ten years ago."

I didn't reply, simply waited—eying him steadily. Neither of us had time to squander on his grief.

Finally, shakily, he said, "She always went to private schools— Burke's, here in the city, then Miss Sherwood's, in Vermont. She always got good grades. Always, even when she was a little girl. Her brother, Bruce, never—" He stopped, glancing at me quickly, almost furtively. Then: "Karen always did well in school. In Radcliffe she was in the top five percent of her class. She's—brilliant." His eyes far away, he blinked again, swallowing hard.

"What did she do after college?" I prodded.

"That—that's when it all happened. After college. She graduated when she was only twenty. Then she went to New York. It was her—first taste of freedom, I suppose. She worked for one of those avant-garde literary magazines for a while; I don't even remember its name. All I remember is the salary they paid her—three hundred seventy-five a month. Her rent, if I remember, was two hundred eighty." Recalling, there was a note of bitterness in his voice.

"How'd she make the rent?"

"On her twenty-first birthday Karen inherited a trust fund," he said, almost reluctantly, "from her grandfather—my wife's father."

"What was the value of that fund, Mr. Manley?"

"Just under four hundred thousand dollars."

Calculating, I said, "So she had more than twenty thousand dollars a year in private income."

"That's correct, Lieutenant. And that's where it all—started. With that money."

"How do you mean?"

"I mean that she started to come apart. Her values, her basic morality, her good common sense—it all just seemed to—" He paused, as though baffled. "It all seemed to disintegrate, virtually from the moment she got that inheritance. Overnight, almost."

"How do you account for the change, Mr. Manley?"

"I can't account for it, Lieutenant. Unless it's drugs. They say that LSD and STP can produce personality changes."

"Was your daughter heavily involved with drugs, Mr. Manley?"

"I—I'm not really sure. I mean, I know she—experimented. I got that much from Bruce, my son. But hell, the majority of kids experiment. They *all* smoke pot. And a lot of them, I understand, try

44

LSD and STP once or twice. And if they're careful—if they quit after the first time or two—they seem to come out of it. So—" He broke off, shaking his head helplessly.

"We come back to the money, then—her inheritance."

For a long moment he didn't reply, but simply stared down at the rosewood desk. His hands, as before, were braced wide apart, as if he were afraid of toppling forward. Then, speaking in a low voice, he said, "We live in a society that worships money. Yet, so help me God, I've seen more people made miserable by money than I've seen made happy. My whole family, from my grandparents right down to my children—they've all had money. And they've all been un-happy."

"Why is that, Mr. Manley?"

"I don't know, Lieutenant. Unless it's the—the magnification factor of money. Everything is more intense. Starker. Everything moves faster. It's like driving a fast car, you can't make any mistakes. It—it's hard to explain. I—I don't know what I'm really saying, even, except that it's all a fraud—a vicious, dishonest farce concocted by overpaid copywriters who really want to be penniless poets. So—" Again he shook his head, then turned his hands palms up on the desk in a small gesture of both supplication and defeat. "So you end up with everything and nothing. Just like everyone else. It's the American way."

"You're right," I answered softly, caught up in his mood. "I was defrauded myself, I'm afraid. A long time ago."

When he looked up to meet my gaze, I saw that his eyes were brimming.

"I've got to go, Lieutenant." He rose. "Will Karen be—" He paused, cleared his throat, then said, "Will she be taken to the morgue?"

"Yessir." I rose with him. "I'll have one of my men meet you at your home. He'll be waiting outside for you. He'll help you—stay with you, as long as you need him."

"Thank you. Are you going to interview the—the members of my family?"

"Yes. I'll give it an hour, though—until you've had a chance to talk with them. Is there just your wife and son?"

He took a handkerchief from his pocket. Looking down at the neatly folded square of gleaming white linen, he said indistinctly, "There is now, Lieutenant. Just my wife and son."

7

The patrolman standing "reporter guard" at the Manleys' front door didn't recognize me. Coldly watching my approach, he was casually smoking a cigarette. When I identified myself, he clumsily shifted the cigarette from his right hand to his left, hastily half-saluting.

A trim, quick-eyed Negro maid led me to a small sitting room in the back of the house. The door was open. A small, stylish woman sat alone in a chintz-covered wing chair. She was dressed in a simple white blouse and gray flannel skirt, the carefully cut, understated morning uniform of the fashionable Pacific Heights matron. She was half-turned away from me, looking out at a magnificent view of the Golden Gate. Her hands were clasped in her lap. Between two gracefully crooked fingers she held a smoldering cigarette. Her neatly coiffured head was held painfully erect. The whole high-style tableau—the woman, the room, the view—all seemed carefully composed, ready for a *Town and Country* photographer.

I introduced myself, hesitated a moment, then sat to face her, uninvited. "I won't take much of your time, Mrs. Manley. I'm sorry I have to be here at all. But I don't have any choice."

Her posture didn't change; her dark, inscrutable eyes didn't shift. Her face was rigid, unrevealing—muscles tautly drawn, pale lips compressed, chin uptilted. Studying her covertly, I found myself irrelevantly wondering whether the Elizabeth Arden perfection of her make-up might be all that kept her face from dissolving into crumpled, ugly, middle-aged grief. Then, more to the point, I wondered whether she'd wept, hearing of her daughter's murder. If she'd been crying, she'd completely repaired the cosmetic damage during the half-hour since Mr. Manley must have left for the morgue.

"What I need from you, Mrs. Manley," I said, "is some idea of who you think might have wanted to kill your daughter. Did she have any enemies, that you know of?"

For a long moment, sitting perfectly motionless, fixedly staring at the view, she didn't stir. Then she lowered her eyes to the cigarette she still held. Finally, with slow, wooden precision, she ground it out in an overflowing crystal ashtray.

Turning only her head, hands gripping the arms of the wing chair, she twisted to face me fully. Her expression was aloof; her features were taut, tightly drawn—thoroughbred lean. Something behind her eyes was dead.

"I didn't know anything about my daughter's life, Lieutenant. Nothing at all. I didn't even know her friends, much less her enemies."

"She was the beneficiary of a sizable trust fund, I understand."
She nodded.

"Can you tell me," I said slowly, "the disposition of that money, now—" I let it go unfinished.

She sighed once, very deeply. "I'm not really sure, Lieutenant. I'd have to consult our lawyer. But the fund was for the children— specifically for the children. Bruce and Karen."

"Does your son have a similar inheritance?"

"Yes, he does. But it's smaller than Karen's, because of his age."

"How much smaller, would you say?"

She frowned, puzzled. Then she began shaking her head. Her gaze was vague, unfocused. I was losing her.

"Can you tell me anything else that might help me, Mrs. Manley?" I pressed. "Can you guess why she might've been killed?"

For a long, lingering moment her dark, dead eyes studied me.

Yet I realized that my question hadn't registered. She was lost—wandering aimlessly somewhere deep inside herself.

Very slowly, very deliberately—still tightly gripping the chair—she turned back to the Golden Gate.

"I'm fifty-two years old," she said in a dull, disembodied monotone, "and I've been sitting in this chair—in this same position—for more than an hour." She paused, again sighing deeply—obviously in shock. Then, in the same trancelike voice: "I don't think I can ever remember sitting in a chair for an hour. Not since I was a little girl, anyhow. Not since I used to read books, during one whole summer—the summer I got orthodontic braces and hated to go outside."

I didn't answer—didn't want to disturb her.

"Just before you came," she was saying, "sitting here, I suddenly realized that I was thinking back over my life—actually reliving the past, the way you're supposed to relive your life when you're dying. It was a—a shock. Introspection isn't my bag, as"—she gulped spasmodically—"as the children say."

"Is your other child here, Mrs. Manley? Now?"

A wry, ironic bitterness worked at her mouth. "Yes," she answered, "Bruce is here. He arrived about a half-hour ago. To"—she smiled faintly—"to comfort me, I imagine. However, I'm sure he'll be leaving soon. If he hasn't left already."

I rose. "I'll see if I can find him. I—I'm very sorry for your loss. If there's anything we can do to help, call me. I'll leave my card with your maid."

She nodded silently. Still with her chin high, she was looking out again at her expensive view, alone.

I found Bruce Manley in the kitchen. He was sitting at a small breakfast table, holding an empty coffee cup. He was a "3-A subject"—average height, average build, average features. His lank sandy hair was worn hippie-length. His complexion was sallow; his drab brown eyes moved indecisively. His mouth was too small, his nose too thin, his chin too weak. His head was set at an odd, forward angle on his scrawny neck. He was dressed in a torn, dirty red and black hunting shirt, faded blue Levi's and black engineer's boots.

Walking the street, his scruffy appearance and slack, sloppy posture would catch the attention of any officer searching for suspects. In the Manley kitchen, against a lavish background of formica, stainless steel and polished wood, he was wildly out of place.

Standing before him, looking him over, I first confirmed his identity, then introduced myself. Watching his sluggish response, I wondered whether Bruce Manley was "softened up"—permanently spaced out: a lost, lonely casualty of the drug culture.

I sat across the table, still looking him over, silently. Quickly he began to fidget, his glance flickering from the coffee cup to my face, then fleetingly around the kitchen, finally returning to the empty cup, which he held as if he were trying to warm both hands. He was swallowing repeatedly—noisily bobbing his prominent Adam's apple.

"You're younger than your sister," I began, pitching my voice to a casual conversational level.

For the first time he looked at me, then nodded jerkily.

"How old are you?" I pressed.

"I'm"—he licked his lips—"I'm twenty-three."

"Your sister was twenty-six."

"Yes."

"Did you see much of your sister?"

"Once in a while," he mumbled, his eyes averted again.

"When was the last time you saw her?"

"I"—he swallowed—"I saw her last night."

With great effort I kept my eyes steady, my voice level and noncommittal as I said, "What time did you see her last night?" My breathing, I realized, was suddenly uneven.

"About eleven o'clock, I guess. I—"

The kitchen door opened. A heavy-set woman in a cook's uniform came into the kitchen. Seeing us, she stopped short, startled, hand on her bulging bosom. Then, turning to the boy, she said heavily, "Hello, Bruce."

His face was expressionless as he looked up at her. "Hello, Florence."

Her eyes were red; she'd been crying, and was ready to begin crying again, soap-opera style. As I drew a long, impatient breath, she turned to me apologetically. "I was just going to—to start something for lunch. It—it's almost noon, and—" Her voice trailed off as she flapped her hands helplessly, looking at Bruce Manley with dampish, chin-quivering sympathy.

I asked her to come back in ten minutes. Then, realizing that I must get Bruce Manley alone, I asked him where he lived. He gave me an address in Buena Vista Heights.

"Do you have a car?" I asked.

"No. My roommate has it. I took a cab."

"I'll drive you home, then." I rose to my feet, standing before him as he obediently rose, stoop-shouldered, listless-seeming.

8

"There it is." He pointed to a vintage shingled house set back from the street. The house, like the neighborhood, had once been comfortably upper-middle-class. But five years ago the Haight-Ashbury had materialized, just down the hill.

We'd hardly spoken during the short drive from Pacific Heights to Buena Vista Heights. Once or twice I'd caught him glancing at me sideways, but I couldn't fathom his expression, or his mood. When I'd expressed sympathy for the loss of his sister, he'd hardly responded, except to sigh petulantly, as if the subject was more exasperating than tragic. Plainly, Bruce Manley was withdrawn and unhappy. But his unhappiness went much deeper than the death of his sister.

"Thanks for the ride," he said shortly, reaching jerkily for the door handle.

"Do you mind if I come in with you? I'd like to ask you about last night, if you've got a few minutes."

He removed his hand from the handle and twisted to face me. His muddy, unhappy brown eyes were unblinking. "What about last night?" His voice was level; his gaze was flat. Suddenly he seemed in full possession of himself.

Strangely, I felt on the defensive. "I'd like you to tell me everything about last night that relates to your sister—when you saw her, where, for how long. Everything."

He blinked with mild vexation, and then began a bored-sounding recital: "I got to her apartment about eleven, as I said. I was with Billy—Billy Mitchell, my roommate. We stayed for about an hour. Maybe an hour and a half."

"So you left not later than twelve-thirty."

"Yes."

"Did you come directly home?"

He nodded, and again seemed totally indifferent—inert, listless. Had I been wrong about the effect of his sister's death? Was he actually in delayed shock?

I couldn't be sure. I couldn't get to him—couldn't find the handle. I couldn't decide whether he was intelligent or dull—on drugs or off drugs—possibly guilty or apparently innocent. His mannerisms and his speech were contradictory. One moment he seemed self-assured; the next moment, vulnerable, indecisive, withdrawn.

"Why'd you visit your sister last night?" I asked. "Any special reason?"

"I went to pick up some grass, Lieutenant." He said it with a kind of wry, resigned defiance.

I wondered whether I'd finally found the handle: a basic indifference to whatever trouble he might cause himself. He was a bleeder, licking greedily at his self-inflicted wounds. In admitting to possession, he was obliquely challenging me to take action against him.

I nodded to the brown-shingled house. "Do you own, or rent?"

"Rent."

"How long have you lived here?"

"About a year."

"What was your previous residence?"

He half-snorted, humorlessly. "A succession of colleges. Europe for six months. Greenwich Village for a year, and Santa Fe for a while."

"That's quite an odyssey."

"You say that like a man who might've been on an odyssey or two himself, Lieutenant." His voice was touched with lazy irony; his eyes slanted toward me with an almost insolent appraisal. The glance could easily have passed from one bar stool to another—in a gay bar.

"Almost everyone goes on an odyssey or two," I answered. "It's just that the routes vary with the bankroll."

"You turn a neat phrase, Lieutenant. I always thought policemen were basically inarticulate. Cruel, right-wing, Irish and inarticulate."

"That description might cover half the cops I know. But that still leaves half."

"Touché."

I allowed a moment to pass, slowing the conversation's pace. The interrogation had slipped into a bantering, abrasive pattern, perfect for my purpose. I didn't want to break his mood.

"I understand," I said, "that both you and your sister have—had—trust funds."

His only response was a watchful nod.

"Hers was about four hundred thousand dollars."

"Yes." His voice was very low.

"Yours is somewhat smaller, I understand."

Sighing with broadly affected boredom, he said, "That's correct. Three hundred thousand smaller, to be exact."

"Yours is a hundred thousand dollars, then."

"Yes."

A hundred thousand at, say, six percent came to six thousand a year. Not much, for someone who liked to travel. I decided to defer the too-obvious question of who would inherit Karen's estate. I had him talking. I wanted to keep him talking.

"I'd like to get back to last night, Bruce. Were both your sister and Mr. Valenti at home?"

"Yes. They were almost always home. They spent most of their time in bed, getting stoned and watching color TV and making love. Except, of course, for the time Valenti spent doing his isometrics, to keep his tummy trim."

"Were they in bed last night?"

"Valenti was. Karen got into something comfortable and came to the door. Then we all went back to the bedroom."

"Was the front door locked when you arrived?"

"I guess so. I didn't try it."

"Did they usually keep their doors locked?"

"I couldn't say."

"Was Valenti nude when you and your roommate entered the bedroom?"

"As much as I could see of him. He didn't treat us to a view of his genitals."

"So the four of you, then, watched TV."

"Yes."

"Do you remember what programs you watched?"

He smiled with a kind of supercilious, tolerant superiority. "It was a movie. *The Glass Key,* I think."

"During that whole time, did your sister and Mr. Valenti stay in bed?"

"Except for when she got me the stuff."

He was insisting. Reluctantly, I said, "The marijuana, you mean."

"Yes."

"How much marijuana did you pick up?"

"A lid."

"Did you buy it?"

"Yes."

"For how much?"

"Fifteen dollars."

"Did you give the money to your sister?"

"No. To Valenti."

"Had you bought marijuana from Valenti in the past?"

"Sure. Two, three times a month. The rumor was that he was trying to make himself financially independent of my sister. Using her money for capital, of course."

Drumming my fingers on the steering wheel, I was looking absently at a small group of shrilly quarreling children. I was thinking, wryly, that I could arrange a pot bust of the Manley-Mitchell premises, and make a few cheap headlines for myself. For some reason, Bruce Manley was almost asking for a pot bust. Why? Was it a false-arrest trap? Was it a need to confess, and suffer—a love-hate relationship with his roommate? Did he want to go to jail with Billy Mitchell, sharing the same peril?

I glanced at Manley, speculating on how he got his sexual kicks.

"Did Valenti deal in drugs on a fairly large scale, would you say?" I asked.

"I have no idea. I just know about the rumors, as I said."

"If he was dealing, it's quite possible that he had drugs on the premises—large quantities of drugs. Cash, too."

"I suppose so. I really wouldn't know."

I nodded, thinking about it. I decided to shift my ground. "Do you know how your sister and Valenti happened to meet?"

"They met in Los Angeles, probably at some wild, wicked party. Which Valenti probably arranged."

"Why do you say that?"

"Because Valenti was a gigolo. No good. Everyone could see it but Karen. Unfortunately, though, Karen wasn't in a very strong bargaining position with men—not, at least, until she came into her inheritance. By then, it was too late; she'd never learned the rules of the game. So she was stuck with people like Valenti. Leeches."

"Did he mistreat your sister?"

"Physically, you mean? Or otherwise?"

"Either way."

"Well, last night, for instance, an ex-girl friend of Valenti's phoned. Everyone could hear her screeching at him. It was a wild scene—really wild. There was Valenti, sitting up in bed, naked, grinning his oily, 1930-style gigolo's smile—smoothing down his stupid patent-leather hair, and smoking a joint while he murmured sweet Latin nothings into the phone. Honest to God, it was like a bad out-of-date movie. Karen was steaming. But at the same time, she was also trying to ignore it—the way dear old Mother presumably taught her."

"What was this ex-girl friend screeching about?"

"According to Valenti, she was consumed with unrequited love.

But that doesn't mean it was true. More likely, she was bugging him for money. According to Karen—who told me about it once when she was stoned—this alleged ex-girl friend actually had Valenti's kid. Which, naturally, Valenti won't admit. Still—" Bruce Manley shrugged languidly.

"Do you know this girl friend's name?"

"Yes. Jane Swanson. She and Valenti apparently met in Las Vegas, which would be their natural habitat. They lived together off and on for two or three years. Jane was a hostess in a casino, which is another word for a free-lance call girl. Valenti, I hear, hired himself out to women, for an hour or a month. Between their separate engagements, they lived together, probably so they could share the rent. It was a beautiful, free relationship."

"Did your sister first meet Valenti in Las Vegas?"

"I don't think so. Presumably, Valenti considered Las Vegas the minor leagues, where he polished his technique. When he felt he was ready—when his accent sounded right in the bathroom, probably—he moved up to Los Angeles. Hollywood."

"And Jane Swanson followed him."

"At a respectful distance. However, as Valenti solidified his hold on Karen, he lengthened the distance between himself and Jane, so that Jane was compelled to take on someone."

"How do you mean?"

"I mean, she's been living with a sometimes bartender named Rawlings—Dave Rawlings, I think."

I'd taken out my notebook, scribbling down the names, places and approximate dates. As I wrote, I glanced at Bruce Manley. He seemed to be tiring rapidly—coasting, perhaps, from an "up" to a "down," losing his grip.

"Have you actually met either Jane Swanson or Dave Rawlings?" I asked.

"I met Jane once," he answered dreamily. "Karen was attending a family funeral, to which I wasn't invited. I stopped by her place to replenish my supply of grass. Jane was there, with Valenti. I mentioned it to Karen. When I did, she told me the whole story. She was pretty upset."

"How did your sister happen to know so much about Valenti's involvement with Jane Swanson?"

He smirked. "She hired a private eye. Karen was like that. She wanted to know the worst."

"Your sister, I gather, wasn't an especially happy person."

"Neither of us is very happy, Lieutenant." His voice was soft, his manner disinterested, remote.

"Your father says it's because you've got too much money."

"Maybe he's right. Or maybe that was his problem, and he just passed it on to us. Maybe the rich shouldn't reproduce—like morons, and other social undesirables."

"Yet you and your sister chose to live in San Francisco, in the same city with your parents."

A spontaneous grimace split his mask of dreamy indifference, revealing a wild, blazing bitterness. His voice was very low, his eyes very bright as he said, "In the first place, Lieutenant, San Francisco's the most exciting city in the world. Furthermore, our presence here was the surest way of getting back at our parents for twenty-odd years of nothing."

"They'd prefer that you were somewhere else, you mean."

"That's it, Lieutenant. Exactly. They live in daily terror of looking up from martinis with the French consul to find Karen or me standing in the doorway. They—" He turned away from me, then blindly wrenched open the door and got out of the cruiser. Leaning in through the window, his venomous voice hardly more than a whisper, he said, "When you find the murderer, Lieutenant, I hope you call me. I want to look in his face. I want to spit on the bastard. Then I want to thank him, for choosing Karen first. Because it could have been me, Lieutenant. For different reasons, by someone else's hand—in a different place, at a different time, it could have been me."

He turned away, stumbling across the sidewalk, banging the sagging wrought-iron gate behind him. I watched him enter his small shingled house, automatically noting that he hadn't unlocked his front door.

9

Still parked in front of the house, I sat motionless behind the wheel, mentally replaying Bruce Manley's final outburst, fixing his strange, bitter phrases in my mind.

Did he actually believe that Karen's murderer could have been his own? Did he believe they'd both been marked for death? Or was he simply indulging himself in bitter, post-adolescent theatrics?

I had no idea—no specific suspicions, no theories. The interview had promised more than it finally delivered. An hour ago I thought I had a suspect. Now I wasn't so sure.

I called in, got Friedman and requested an address check on Jane Swanson and Dave Rawlings. Grumbling sourly about the suddenly skyrocketing homicide rate, Friedman instructed me to come in for a two P.M. conference with Captain Kreiger. I agreed, then asked for a surveillance on the Bruce Manley-Billy Mitchell residence. I had just said goodbye to Friedman and was checking into the communications net when I saw a white Volkswagen, this year's or last's, pulling to a stop across the street. I watched a tall, lean, restless-moving young man get out of the car and cross in front of me, heading for the shingled house. Calling out quickly, I moved to intercept him at the iron gate.

"Mr. Mitchell?" I asked. "Billy Mitchell?"

His slightly upslanted, wolfish gray eyes were level with my own. I saw the eyes narrow as I reached into my side pocket and showed him the shield, introducing myself.

Mitchell gave way before me, an involuntary half-step. He was instantly on guard. His eyes moved covertly toward the house, then quickly back to me. His face was lean, dominated by a tight yet mobile mouth, high cheekbones and pale, predatory oriental eyes. He wore slim leather trousers and heavy boots, a bright paisley shirt open to the waist. A blue bandanna was knotted flamboyantly at his throat. His reddish-blond hair was medium long, carefully cut. He was in his middle twenties. He looked intelligent, ill-tempered and smugly self-satisfied.

"What can I do for you?" He was arranging his stance in a studied, loose-jointed effort to appear sardonic, nonchalant.

I bluntly described the double murder, testing his response. His eyes flickered, but his lean, gracefully poised body remained relaxed. He seemed to be coolly studying me.

When I'd finished my brief accounting of the crime, he allowed a moment to pass, then said, "That chick was a victim type. Like she was asking for it. Masochism is the female thing, but she wore it out. Really ran it into the ground. All the way into the ground, deep and dead."

"You knew her pretty well, then."

He shrugged. "I saw her twice. Maybe three times. But she was sick, man. You could see it. She had these calf eyes. And she hugged herself whenever someone stuck her real good. Which is what Valenti was good at: sticking her."

I studied him a moment, then said quietly, "You're quite a philosopher." Moving my head to the cruiser, I said, "Would you mind coming over to the car for a minute or two? I'd like to double-check a few things."

"What kind of things?" He wasn't moving.

I turned to face him squarely. "Your movements last night."

"Hmm." He folded his arms. Then: "I don't get it."

"There's nothing to get, Mitchell. I'm asking you, as a matter of information, what you were doing last night. From, say, ten o'clock until midnight."

"Are you telling me that I'm a suspect, or something? Is that where you're going with this?"

I moved slightly away from him, instinctively giving myself room—aware that the muscles of my back and thighs were tightening.

"If you were a suspect, Mitchell, I'd've already given you your constitutional rights, and we'd probably be on our way downtown." I paused, letting it sink in before saying, "I'm asking you a simple, direct question. If you don't want to answer, then we'll probably have to change the script." I gestured toward him with my right hand, palm up, invitingly. "So it's up to you: the hard way or the easy way."

"Christ, it's just like on the boob tube. *Dragnet.* Taaa da *dum, dum.*" It was the *Dragnet* theme.

I didn't answer.

With lower lip protruding, he exhaled suddenly, ruffling his reddish hair. It was a strangely childlike, innocent mannerism.

"I went over to Karen's," he said abruptly, "with Brucie boy. We got there about eleven, and split about twelve-thirty."

"What happened then?"

"We came home. We went directly home. We didn't pass Go."

I nodded thoughtfully, studying him. Then: "What d'you do for a living, Mitchell?"

"Different things."

"What kind of things?"

He raised his shoulders in a languid shrug. "I've only been out of the army for a year. I've just been making the scene—hanging loose."

"Were you a draftee?"

He nodded.

"Where's your home?"

"New York. Albany, New York."

"What's your father's name?"

"What's my father got to do with it?"

I drew a long, slow breath, glanced up and down the street and then stepped closer to him. In a low, tight voice I said, "I've got a double murder to investigate, Mitchell—a very important murder, involving very important people. I don't know much about the murder. We don't know the motive yet, but it'll probably turn out that the motive has something to do with gain. And if that's the way it turns out, we'll be looking for people with the most to gain. And someone like yourself—someone with nothing to lose and maybe lots to gain—you could interest us a lot. So that's why I was asking you for your father's name. Maybe he's a capitalist, for instance, who sends you five hundred dollars a month, just to stay in California. If that's the case, we'd like to know about it."

He snorted, amused at some private little joke. "My father was a peddler, Lieutenant. A round-shouldered, soft-talking, sick-smiling peddler, selling wholesale draperies. Unfortunately, he wasn't a very good peddler. So he started drinking, and my mother started working. When I was seven years old, Mummy kicked Daddy out of the house. Literally. Whereupon Daddy became a bum—a wino, in fact. When I was a bad little boy—or a bad big boy—my mother would tell me that I'd grow up to be just like Daddy."

I sighed involuntarily, pausing a moment—secretly assessing the unwitting damage he'd done me. He'd come incredibly close. He could have caught me with a sucker punch, and done less damage. I hadn't quite been a drunk; I hadn't quite abandoned the children. I'd merely left them to their mother—their sleek, golden predator-of-a-mother, so breathtakingly perfect that she seemed unreal even in memory. She'd—

"—isn't exactly a capitalist, either," he was saying. "Unless you figure a four-chair beauty shop is big business. Still, Mummy isn't hurting."

I blinked, then automatically asked, "Do you have an allowance?"

"No."

"How do you live, then?"

"I live off Bruce."

I nodded, thought about it, and then decided to say, "That doesn't make you much different from Valenti."

Forcing a smile, he said, "Nobody's perfect, Lieutenant. Everyone's out for a little more than he's got. Take the Manleys, for instance. They've got it all, but they still want more. Even the old man, Mister High Society—Mister Perfection. Turn over his rock, and you'd be surprised what you'd find. In fact—" His mouth twisted in a derisive, satanic grin. "In fact, if you're looking for suspects, you should be talking to the old man, not Bruce."

"I don't think you know what you're talking about, Mitchell." I said it flatly, hopefully to goad him into continuing.

"Yeah? Well, ask Walter J. Manley about a girl named Candice Weiss. She's a beautifully stacked chick who happens to take money from Sugar Daddy Walter. Then she turns around and buys stuff from Valenti. So you can imagine the scene. There's Walter J. Manley, accusing his daughter of loose living. And there's Karen, accusing Daddy right back in his teeth. And there's Valenti, smiling."

For a long, silent moment I studied him, watching his grin widen.

"What's the matter, Lieutenant?" he asked softly. "Are you a little shook, to think that you might have to pick on someone a little bigger than you are?"

Ignoring the remark, I took down his mother's name and address, then instructed him not to leave town.

"It's beginning to sound like I should get a lawyer," he said. "I think I will get one, in fact. I'll tell Bruce to get one, too. Or maybe we can share one with his father. We could cut expenses."

"Use your own judgment, Mitchell. Think it over. And while you're thinking, you might give a little thought to the kind of life you're living. I see a lot of people like you—you're my stock in trade. Nothing surprises you; nothing shocks you. Nothing much matters, really. You'll try almost anything, once. You're probably involved with drugs. If you are, you'll find that drugs plus that chip on your shoulder are a bad combination." I flipped the notebook closed, returning it to my pocket, clicking my ballpoint pen. "You might also mention my little sermon to Bruce Manley. You'll probably both get a chuckle out of it. Unfortunately."

I got in the cruiser and drove off without looking back, already behind schedule for the captain's meeting.

10

I knocked once on Kreiger's door, then turned the knob. As I took the armchair left empty for me, I saw Kreiger glance pointedly at his watch. The time was five minutes after two, and the captain didn't approve. I wouldn't have approved either if I'd called the meeting.

Canelli, Markham and Friedman sat around Kreiger's oversized gray-steel desk. Each man nodded at me, mumbling a greeting that matched his rank. Friedman was smoking a cigar, Markham a cigarette. Canelli was doodling, drawing an elaborate Christmas tree. I placed two manila file folders on the desk, drawing up my chair. Canelli laboriously hunched his chair aside, making room. His elbow caught the doodle of the Christmas tree, sailing it to the floor close beside the captain's chair.

Kreiger glanced down at the drawing, sighed once and then turned to me. "How about leading off, Frank? Let's see what we've got. Start with Draper."

Referring to notes, I outlined the case in two minutes or less, focusing my monologue on Kreiger. His pale Prussian eyes were expressionless. He sat stolidly in his chair, big hands clasped quietly together on the desk before him. His curly blond hair, still thick at forty-four, was close-cropped. Kreiger was a squared-off, calm, precise man. I'd first met him more than twenty years ago, in the army.

We'd been on a brief football-player's gravy train, stationed at Fort Monmouth. He'd tackled me hard enough to flatten me on the hard turf of an ill-prepared practice field. He'd looked down at me for an expressionless, reflective moment, then noncommittally helped me to my feet. The incident was typical of Kreiger: tough and efficient, he'd first had his way. Then, unsmilingly generous, he'd repaired the damage—asking nothing, revealing nothing, expecting nothing.

When I'd finished talking, Kreiger made a few brief notes, then turned to Markham. "Anything to add, Jerry?"

"A couple of things." Markham's voice was subdued, yet subtly smug. He'd always been good on the street. Now he was learning to handle himself in the captain's office. "The lab men found a smear of blood on the front door," Markham said, "undoubtedly left by Mr. Draper when he went inside to phone us, after he discovered the body."

"Did he admit to touching the body?"

"Not to me, he didn't," Markham said, turning inquiringly to me.

"It's unclear," I said. "My impression was that he didn't remember much. Anyhow, the point wasn't established."

"He could've been purposely evasive," Kreiger said. Then, to Markham: "What else besides the blood smear?"

"An unclassified print on the handle of the garage door. Not Mrs. Draper's either. Or Mr. Draper's."

"Is it a good print?"

"A dream. A thumbprint. Right thumb. It's already in Washington and Sacramento. The print was made *over* prints of both Mr. and Mrs. Draper. So it's exceptionally clear."

"Good," Kreiger said, inclining his head gravely. "What else?"

"I questioned the little girl. She slept right through the murder, apparently. But she said that her parents were fighting yesterday afternoon."

"How do you rate her as a witness?"

Markham shrugged. "She's only seven. Personally, I've never had much luck with kids that age. Twelve, yes. Seven, no."

Kreiger was thoughtfully making notes on a large legal-size pad.

Finally he said, "The way I understand it, then, we're going in three directions: we've got Draper as a possibility, and we've got this kid Dan Haywood. But mostly we're going on the third possibility: that a mugger with either robbery or rape in mind did the job. Which would tie in with what the Haywood kid says about the black man he saw. Assuming, of course, that the Haywood kid isn't lying." He looked from Markham to me. "Anything else?" He said it crisply, plainly anxious to get on to the Manley homicide.

"That garage door handle should take beautiful prints," I said slowly, ignoring Kreiger's frown as I turned to Markham.

"It did."

"There were three sets, you say: Mr. and Mrs. Draper's and the unclassified set on top. Right?"

Markham nodded. His dark eyes were alert as he tried to guess my point.

"Which set was next?"

He frowned.

"It should be Mrs. Draper's," I said. "Her husband didn't touch the outside handle that night, according to both versions of his story. He pushed the door up, from the inside. He discovered his wife's body. Then he left the door up, no matter which way he entered the house. That much is for sure. So his prints should be last. Underneath the other two."

"I'll check," Markham said shortly.

"You might also be sure the lab goes over the inside handle of the garage door. On that handle, if Draper's telling the truth, his prints should be on top."

"I'll check that, too," came the grudging reply.

I nodded, unwilling to press him further in public, even though I wanted a better picture of Draper's precise movements after discovering the body.

I turned to Kreiger. "You want to get to the Manley thing?"

Glancing at his watch, he nodded impassively. This time referring to my notes, I carefully summed up my information. As I talked, the other four men became more attentive. The Manley case meant prestige, publicity, possible promotion. Something for everyone.

When I'd finished, Friedman shook his head elaborately, mock-dolefully. "You'll have to do better than that, Lieutenant. So far, as suspects, you've come up with a millionaire and a millionaire's son. At that rate, you and I will be out dodging bullets, while Canelli and Markham sit behind our scarred oak desks."

Unsmiling, Kreiger asked Canelli for a summary of late developments at the scene of the crime. Canelli cleared his throat, frowning with earnest, sweat-sheened concentration. It would be years before Canelli would learn to handle himself in the captain's office.

"Well," Canelli began, "I was just down to the lab before I came here, and the lab—" He swallowed, still frowning earnestly, looking first to me, then to the captain. "Or maybe you read the lab reports already."

"Never mind," Kreiger said. "Tell us about it. I've read the report. But Lieutenant Friedman hasn't."

"I haven't either," I said. "I just got here."

"Oh. Well—" Again he swallowed. "Well, the lab came up with something like nine sets of prints, so it's going to take a little while to sort it all out. So far, all they can eliminate are prints from the two victims, plus the cleaning lady. Which leaves six. So—" He cleared his throat. "So that's where we are on prints. About the bullets, out of four shots, we don't have a damn thing. I mean, they all went right on through; they're all messed up. You can't tell the lands from the grooves. But the lab figures the gun was probably either a .357 Magnum or a .38."

"Did they recover the bullets?" Friedman asked, shifting his bulk to flick his cigar ashes, then subsiding with a sigh.

"Yep. All four of them. All in the wall. It's a wood-paneled wall, and one of the slugs went all the way through that wall, and almost through the kitchen wall. It's bulging out, like a boil, or something. So you know it was a pretty powerful gun. Like the lab says."

"How about money and drugs on the premises?" I asked.

"We found two hundred thirty dollars in a bedroom bureau, in Valenti's wallet. Which seems to rule out robbery, unless they only took the real big stuff. The girl had about twenty dollars in her purse.

So far, we haven't found anything but a kilo of marijuana. But we're still looking."

"Have you and Culligan been able to reconstruct the murderer's movements from any physical evidence?"

"More or less. It looks like the murderer must've come in through the front service door, which wasn't locked. From there, he had to go alongside the house and back to the garden. Then it looks like he jimmied the back door. It's just a spring lock, so it didn't take much. Also, there's some marks along the lock, according to Estes from the lab. I couldn't see any marks myself; I figured it was a celluloid job. Still—"

"Then what happened?" Kreiger interrupted.

"Well—" Canelli lifted his hands, palms up. "He just went in and did the job, it looks like."

"What about that talcum powder?" I asked.

Canelli snapped his fingers ruefully, loudly clicking his teeth. "I *knew* I was forgetting something. Estes claims he followed it right from the bedroom into the kitchen and out onto the back porch and then alongside the house to the service door, and out to the sidewalk. Which is a pretty good reason for figuring that's the way the murderer came, figuring that he left the same way he came. *If* Estes is right. Personally, I think that those lab guys figure they know more than they really know. I mean, they find a couple of specks of suspicious-looking dust, or something, and right away they think they've got the whole case solved."

"It's evidence, though," Friedman said gently. "It impresses juries." He eyed Canelli for a moment, then said in the same soft, speculative voice, "Maybe, unconsciously, you're jealous of Estes' willowy physique. Have you ever thought about that?" He moved his cigar toward me. "I used to have similar feelings concerning Lieutenant Hastings, even when he was a sergeant. I used to think it was professional jealousy. Then I realized that it was his thirty-four-inch waist. Not to mention his forty-four-inch chest."

"What about witnesses?" I asked Canelli.

Frowning dubiously at Friedman, Canelli said absently, "Yeah. Well, we turned up quite a few. I mean, the M.E. said the murder was probably committed between midnight and three A.M. And the upstairs neighbor thought he heard shots about two A.M., which would tie in with what the M.E. said. So me and Culligan, we—" He paused for breath. Watching him, Friedman rolled his eyes briefly upward, elaborately exhaling. "We went on the theory that we should be looking for people out on the street about then. About two. And we probably found a dozen people, which kind of surprised me. Of course, it's the holiday season, and all. But anyhow—" Again he paused, breathing deeply.

"This suspense," Friedman muttered, "is almost unbearable."

"Anyhow, we got two or three pretty good witnesses," Canelli continued, apparently oblivious to his sardonic superior, "who all came up with a late-model Volkswagen bug, white, that was parked in the area for maybe a half-hour or so around two o'clock, with someone inside. So we started—"

At the word "Volkswagen," I felt myself stiffen.

"Bruce Manley," I said, "has a white VW bug."

Kreiger's expression, typically, didn't change. Friedman, typically, whistled reflectively through his teeth. "This," he said, "is what the manual calls a 'potentially significant intersection of seemingly random events.' It's also the answer to a city editor's erotic fantasies."

Kreiger was slowly, precisely tapping his pad of paper with a long yellow pencil. His pale blue eyes were very remote. "We've got to have that car for a lab check," he said. "And we've got to keep it quiet. I don't want the papers to smell a thing."

"This Bruce Manley doesn't sound too sharp," Friedman said thoughtfully. "Maybe we can con him."

"We can't con Billy Mitchell, though," I replied. "Take my word for it."

"We'll just have to play it straight," Kreiger said quietly. "Give Bruce Manley the old wheeze: a car answering the description of his was seen at the scene. For his own good, we want to eliminate his, to clear him. Hell, there must be a thousand cars like that in the city. More than a thousand, maybe. Tell him that; make it sound like a— an amusing coincidence."

"Ho, ho," Friedman interjected dryly.

"What if he doesn't want to cooperate," I asked, "and goes for a lawyer? If he contacts his father, there'll be a lawyer down here in five minutes. Followed by reporters."

Kreiger answered, "We don't have any choice, Frank. We've got to have the car for an hour, with or without the kid's permission. We can't—"

"Why don't we steal it?" Friedman asked blandly.

"What?"

"Why not? I'll go interview Bruce and his buddy. Haskell, from Auto Theft, can do the job while I'm conducting my three-ring interrogation. If Haskell gets caught, we can stage an arrest. I could be the hero. Either way, we'd come up heroes. When the car's reported missing, we'll recover it within the hour."

"If we wait until tonight," I said, "we might even be able to get it back undetected. Then we could—"

"Are you two out of your heads?" Kreiger's lips were tight with the effort of keeping his voice level. "You'll get us all—"

"I could pretend that I don't know Frank has already interviewed him," Friedman interrupted smoothly. "Besides, Haskell's cool. Not only that, he looks more like a crook than a cop. It's a breeze. He could even pretend to be repossessing the car for a bank. I'd leave that part up to him."

"Repossessing proceedings could be libelous," Kreiger snapped. Then, thoughtfully, he added, "A fake theft is better than repossessing."

Friedman looked at me, careful that Kreiger didn't see his smug leer. Canelli seemed embarrassed, as if he were very young, listening to the older boys telling dirty jokes.

In a few minutes we'd fixed the details, deciding to steal the car as soon as possible, hopefully to return it after dark, now less than three hours away. Meanwhile, I would take Canelli and try to interview Jane Swanson and her friend Dave Rawlings. Then, alone, I'd interview Walter Manley.

When the heist was settled, Kreiger abruptly announced that he was going to have a cup of coffee—alone.

11

Canelli swung the cruiser to the curb, switching off the ignition and radio. We sat silently for a moment, surveying the run-down building in which Rawlings' apartment had finally been located. I yawned, stretching. We should have taken time for a cup of coffee.

Canelli cleared his throat, hesitated, and finally said, "Can I ask you something, Lieutenant?"

"Sure." I threw my half-smoked cigarette out the window and turned to face him. For more than a year I'd been trying to quit smoking. I was down to half a pack of half-smoked cigarettes each day.

"Does Lieutenant Friedman have anything against me?"

I smiled. "Yes, he does. He has your waistline against you. Because your waistline reminds him of his waistline. Between the two of you, you've got the whole Bureau jogging twice a week. And Lieutenant Friedman hates exercise."

His guileless relief was almost comical. I'd often wondered how Canelli managed to make Inspector, his incredible luck notwithstanding. Kreiger ran a tight ship. Performance was the first criterion, but appearance and presence counted, too. Kreiger had his own ideas about how an inspector should look and act.

"Can I ask you something else?" he was saying, this time more tentatively.

"All right."

"Well—" He cleared his throat. "Is it really true that you played pro ball for the Lions? I mean, I don't follow football much. Not the older players, anyhow. So—" He broke off. Too late.

I sighed. Then, resigned, I recited: "I played two years on a football scholarship at Stanford, after the war. I got honorable mention in my senior year. I played four years with the Lions, usually as a second-string wingback—a utility man. I was no hero, and I didn't make much money. End of the story."

He nodded, hesitated, then said, "About saying 'older players,' Lieutenant, I—"

"You meant what you said, Canelli. Don't worry. One lieutenant sore at you is enough. More than enough, once Friedman starts jogging. Come on—" I opened the door. "Let's see what Jane Swanson has to say."

I pushed the bell a third time, then pressed my ear gingerly to the door. I could hear the soft sounds of movement within. Should I have sent Canelli to cover the back, playing the percentages? Had they . . . ?

Footsteps were approaching. As the door opened on a chain, I glanced at my watch. The time was 3:45.

"Yes, what is it?" The woman's voice was thick with sleep, drowsily resentful.

I identified myself, verified her identity as Jane Swanson, and asked to be let into the apartment.

"What's it all about?" she asked. But the sudden tightness in her voice betrayed her. She knew.

A good detective, like a good door-to-door salesman, never transacts business in hallways. Finally, pretending exasperation, she let us inside. The door, I noticed, was secured by two chains and two locks.

Both the girl and the apartment were about what I'd expected. The girl was perhaps thirty. Tight magenta stretch slacks and a not-quite-clean print blouse revealed a figure just beginning to spread and sag. Her long brown hair hung tangled about her shoulders; her bare feet padded heavily on the scarred entryway floor. The slow, lazily suggestive swing of her hips seemed somehow more slatternly than sensuous—more listless than lustful.

The dark, stale-smelling apartment was crammed with cheap modern furniture. Discarded clothing, newspapers and movie magazines littered every chair. Children's toys completed the ruin. From a portable TV came the insinuating bleat of a daytime quizmaster. I stepped to the TV and turned down the volume, purposely not asking permission. Then I took a long moment to look around.

The two-bedroom apartment would rent for about a hundred thirty a month, I decided. The neighborhood was marginal, the building probably thirty years old. The kitchen appliances were badly chipped. The bathroom was dingy. A small aluminum Christmas tree had been placed on a sheet-draped table and set before the living room's single window.

"Here—" She cleared the couch of newspapers, a child's sweater and an empty 7-Up bottle. "Sit here." She surveyed the room for a brief, frowning moment before muttering, "I was taking a nap while Jerry and Dave are out. It's the only time I get to myself, between the two of them." She sat in a chocolate-colored plastic armchair, the room's most comfortable piece of furniture. She immediately began picking at the chair's arm with long carmine fingernails, avoiding my eyes, biting at her sullen, pouting lips, painted a matching carmine. Her features were boldly drawn: dark eyebrows, dark eyes, a wide jaw and mouth, straight nose.

"Is Jerry your son?" I began.

She nodded petulantly, then suddenly shifted in the plastic chair, impatiently recrossing her legs. Finally, looking at me directly, she said abruptly, "It's about Valenti, isn't it?"

"Yes, it is. We understand that you phoned him late last night."

"Wh—what?" Her dark eyes widened, then narrowed. "Who the h— Who told you that?" Her voice was raggedly aggressive. Her body, suddenly tensed, arched forward in the chair.

"There were people present at his end, Miss Swanson," I said. "Roberto Valenti was heard to state, by two witnesses, that you called him late in the evening."

"Well, whoever they are," she answered promptly, "they're damned liars. What would I be calling him for? I haven't seen him for—hell, months."

"Did you ever visit him at twenty-seven thirty-one Jackson Street?"

"Well—" Her eyes slid aside.

"How often? Think, Miss Swanson. It's important." I said it gravely, slowly, somberly holding her eye.

Uncertainty now tugged at the brash defiance in her face, revealing a quick flicker of apprehension. Head-to-head, she was a quick-tempered brawler. But she couldn't handle innuendos, or lingering doubt.

"What's so important about it?" For the first time her glance sought Canelli. I saw her look him swiftly up and down with the lazy, expert eyes of a hooker. Then, returning her bold gaze to me, she said, "What're you trying to pull, anyhow?" But her tone seemed almost plaintive now. Watching her slipping into an aggrieved role of outraged innocence, I was suddenly almost sure that she'd once been arrested. Somewhere, sometime, an anonymous cop had made my next half-hour a little easier. Someone had gotten to her—maybe with a fist in an alleyway, maybe with long, sweating hours in an interrogation room. Or maybe she'd been taken, forced to pay off, in cash and in bed. It happens. Often. Everyone thumps on a hooker.

"I'm not trying to 'pull' anything, Miss Swanson. You say you didn't phone Valenti last night. I accept that, for the time being, anyhow. Now I want to know how many times in the past six months you visited him at Miss Manley's apartment."

Her eyes fell. Still gnawing at her lips, frowning pettishly, she muttered, "Twice." Her voice was very low. Defeated, finally.

"Why didn't you want to tell us?" Canelli asked.

Staring down at the plastic arm, she muttered, "You should be able to figure that out, for Christ's sake."

"You didn't want Dave Rawlings to know," I said.

She nodded.

"All right, fine," I said. "That's what we want: answers. The truth. Clear?"

She didn't respond—again shifting in the chair, again recrossing her legs. I allowed myself a brief glance at the tight magenta creases gathered at her crotch. Then: "What was the purpose of these two visits, Miss Swanson?"

"W—what'd you mean?"

"Just what I say: why'd you visit Valenti? You must've had a reason."

"Sure I did. I wanted to see him. Talk over old times. We used to go around together a few years ago." As she said it she looked at me with transparent speculation, gauging the effect of her seemingly spontaneous spasm of honesty.

"Did you ask him for money?"

Her startled sidelong glance was all the answer I needed.

"How much money, Miss Swanson? How much did you—" A key rattled in the lock. Canelli and I exchanged a glance. Nodding to him and moving my head toward the hallway, I said to Jane Swanson, "I'm going to ask you to go into a separate room with Inspector Canelli. I want you to—"

A dark, solemn-eyed boy was standing in the living-room doorway, silently eying us with the shrewd, calculating hostility of a slum urchin. Behind him stood a thick-set, dark man of about thirty-five. The man's sullen watchfulness mirrored the boy's. I rose, made the introductions, showed the shield and quietly suggested that Canelli take the boy and the mother with him. Immediately.

The boy went to stand impassively at his mother's side, staring up at Canelli. The woman reached out absently to touch the boy's forearm with her red-tipped fingers. Her eyes were swinging uncertainly between Dave Rawlings and myself.

Rawlings moved a bandy-legged, belligerent step into the room, standing glowering before me. He was a short, swarthy man with the self-conscious, narcissistic good looks of a Hollywood bit player. Watching him, waiting for him to speak, I thought fleetingly about the Los Angeles–Las Vegas glitter in Valenti's past—the neon-tinted, love-for-hire illusions that produced the three of them: Valenti, Jane Swanson and Dave Rawlings.

"What's going on here, anyhow?" Rawlings was asking.

"Karen Manley and Roberto Valenti were murdered last night," I said. "We're checking into it." I turned to Canelli, gesturing again toward the hallway. I wanted to separate the two subjects before one of them remembered his rights.

"Are you telling me," Rawlings said, "that you think Jane did it, or something?"

"No, I'm not, Mr. Rawlings. But I *am* telling you that she may have information that could help us solve a double homicide. I'm also telling you that you're breaking the law if you make it difficult for us to get that information."

"You gotta have a warrant, though. You can't just—"

"We're not searching the premises, Rawlings. And Miss Swanson invited us inside." I turned my back on him. The woman was on her feet, irresolutely eying the hallway. The boy stood beside her like a small, baleful lover.

Finally, tugging the boy impatiently along, she led the way to the first bedroom on the left. Canelli followed, closing the door behind them.

"Sit down, Mr. Rawlings."

"I'll stand. At least, until I know what's happening around here." He spread his legs, folding his arms belligerently, unconsciously bunching his shoulders—posing. I could imagine him at the beach, rippling his muscles, fondly oiling himself, frowning down at a small role of midriff fat.

I turned to face him fully. Suddenly I didn't like him. Just as suddenly, I wished that I could permit myself the pleasure of telling him so. Instead, in an even voice, I said, "Do you mind telling me whether you were here last night?"

"Why're you asking?" His dark, insolent eyes met mine squarely. He was going to play the tough guy.

"I've already told you, Rawlings: we're here checking background information that could help us with our investigation. Miss Swanson knew Roberto Valenti. She's already given us some of the information we're after. I want you to verify that information." I spread my hands, trying to look pleasant. "It's as simple as that. No one's trying to hassle you. We're looking for leads. Maybe you can help."

He looked at me for a long, silent moment. Then, with a single sudden, irritable movement, he drew off his windbreaker and sat down hard in the brown plastic chair, angrily tossing the windbreaker on the couch. Sure enough, his arms and shoulders bulged with gymnasium muscles.

Not changing my expression, I sat on the couch beside the windbreaker. "Were you here last night?" I asked again.

"Until about eleven," he answered grudgingly, looking past me with blank eyes.

"You went out at eleven?"

He nodded, insolently exaggerating the movement, allowing his eyes to close briefly.

"Where did you go?"

He looked at me, snorted, and then said resentfully, "I just went out. It was my night off, and it got too—heavy around here. I drove for a half-hour, maybe. Then I had a couple of drinks. Then I came on back. Period."

"Did you and Jane argue? Is that what you're saying?"

Again he bobbed his head sullenly.

"You're a bartender, is that right?"

"Right. I work at the Interlude. In North Beach. Last night was my night off."

I paused, studying him. If he was telling the truth about last night, he couldn't help me either confirm or deny Jane's story. She would have called Valenti after Rawlings left.

"Is the Interlude a pretty good place to work?"

He studied me, making up his mind about the new, conversational tone in my voice. Finally, grudgingly, he said, "It's all right. For San Francisco."

"Don't you like San Francisco?"

"No."

"Los Angeles, then."

His eyes narrowed. "Yeah, Los Angeles. Las Vegas, too. Any place but San Francisco."

I raised my shoulders with an indifferent, everyone-to-his-own-taste gesture that I didn't feel. Then, casually, I asked, "What was Jane doing when you left last night?"

He smiled bitterly. "She was getting ready for bed, which she probably told you."

"That doesn't sound like much of an argument."

"Except that she was getting ready to go to bed with the kid. Which happens, as a matter of fact, to be what the argument was about in the first place." He mouthed a long, sibilant "s-h-h-h," letting the "it" go lewdly unsaid. His eyes snapped with suppressed fury as he turned away from me to glare at the far wall. "Women." He spat viciously.

"Is Jane divorced?" As I said it, I kept my voice neutral, merely curious, hoping his anger would start him talking.

He snorted. "She was never married."

I decided not to press the point, asking instead, "How long have the two of you been together?"

"Too long."

"Answer the question, Rawlings." I put an edge on my voice.

"Almost a year."

"And before that she was with Valenti."

He didn't reply.

"She *was* with Valenti. We already know about it."

Again no response. But his eyes were smoldering, his fists clenched. His forearms were corded.

"How many times," I asked softly, "had Jane and Valenti seen each other in the past six months?"

His eyes flashed to my face. "How many times do *you* say?"

"I'm asking the questions, Rawlings."

"None, that's how many times," came the quick, angry response. "Zero."

I sank back, relaxed, against the couch, folding my arms and looking at him with a deliberate expression of amused, ironic sympathy.

"Zero," he repeated. "And if you say different, you're a—" He twisted in the chair, turning away, elaborately ignoring me.

I decided to turn up the heat. "It's not what I say, Rawlings. It's what she says—what she freely admits."

"You're a f— you're a liar. You're trying to—to—" He clamped his jaw down hard on the rest of it.

I got to my feet, went to the bedroom door and softly knocked. "Would you come out here a minute, Miss Swanson? The boy can stay there, with Inspector Canelli."

She came out almost immediately. Her back was straight, her eyes alert, defiant. She gave me a brief, vicious look, then walked ahead of me into the living room, casting at Rawlings the same look she'd thrown at me.

"Well, what's wrong with you?" she asked Rawlings. "What're you looking at, anyhow?"

"I'd hate to say. You wouldn't like the sound of it."

"What's *that* supposed to mean?"

"It's supposed to mean that he says—" Rawlings moved his head toward me, still with his gaze locked in hers. "He says you've been seeing Valenti."

She looked once at me, her eyes round with wordless fury. Then she raised her shoulders in a slow, taunting gesture of utter indifference. "If you'd've asked me, I'd've told you. But you never asked. You—"

He was on his feet. In two swift strides he'd reached her. They stood face to face, fists clenched, oblivious of me. Rawlings' voice was a low, furious whisper. "I've been working my goddamn ass off in this crummy town, bringing the money home to you and that kid—*his* kid. And you're running off screwing him, while I—"

She laughed in his face—a high, harsh, vicious sound that flayed at him like a whip. "A girl's got to have *some* fun. I mean, here I am, stuck with a kid and a so-called man. I'm not turning any tricks any more. You're too goddamn pure for that. So I gotta—"

He drew back his arm, ready to backhand her. Eyes bright, rigid with hatred, she screamed into his face, "Go ahead, you son of a bitch. You're no good for anything else. So you might as well—"

"Hold it, Rawlings. Sit down." I grabbed his wrist. He twisted away, violently. I stayed with the wrist, twisting, pinning the arm behind his back. "Go limp, Rawlings, or spend the night in jail."

"I'd rather be in jail than here," he said hoarsely.

"Sit down." I shoved him toward the brown plastic chair. Then, to Jane Swanson: "I want you to come downtown with us, Miss Swanson. I want a signed statement. The boy can stay with him—" I nodded to Rawlings. "It'll take about an hour."

"Sure," Rawlings shouted, "take her away. And sure, leave the goddamn kid. He spends most of his time with me anyway. She— she—" He didn't finish it, but sat shaking his head like a groggy fighter between rounds, furiously opening and closing his mouth. Finally: "If you want any evidence against her, just ask. I'll be happy to oblige."

Ignoring him, I propelled her by one indignantly bucking elbow to the closet. With my free hand I tapped on the bedroom door.

12

I asked Jane Swanson to get into the front seat of the cruiser. Drawing Canelli aside, I instructed him to take the woman downtown, brief Friedman, then ask Friedman to assist in a complete interrogation. I would phone Friedman with my own information and suggestions. Meanwhile I'd interrogate someone in the area who knew Jane Swanson and Dave Rawlings, trying for a corroboration of their movements last night.

"Shall I come back for you, or what?" Canelli asked.

"No. I'll call for a radio car. When you finish with Swanson, drive her back here. Incidentally, find out what kind of a car she or Rawlings drives. Verify it with DMV. Then, if nothing much is doing here, you might stand by at the office. I want to interview Walter Manley alone, but I might need you later. I'll let you know."

"Right."

"How's Swanson look to you?"

"Tough," he said ruefully. "A real tough one."

I smiled, half-waving goodbye. At a corner drugstore I found a phone booth. Belatedly, I realized that Friedman was probably still out on his car heist. But in a half minute he came on the phone.

"Did you get the car?" I asked.

"Of course. No sweat. Brucie Boy and Billy Boy must've bucked themselves up with a couple of joints after they talked to you

—maybe something heavier. Actually, it was a very profitable interview. Mitchell, particularly, is so entranced with the snotty sound of his own nasal voice—and so entranced with the idea of entrancing Brucie Boy—that he just can't keep himself from talking."

"You're rambling on like Canelli," I said dryly. "I'm out here in the cold, you know, trying to solve a vicious double murder."

"Yeah. Well, briefly, Mitchell gave me a name. Al Goodfellow, San Francisco's noted narcotics wholesaler."

"Was Goodfellow supplying Valenti?"

"According to Mitchell. In pretty good quantities, too. Junk. All junk. And, still according to Mitchell, Valenti got himself spread a little thin financially, and Goodfellow was getting a little uptight about it. Valenti apparently decided he was going to introduce a credit system among his circle of sophisticated, affluent junkies. If it worked for Diner's Club, he probably reasoned, it would work for him. But it didn't. And Goodfellow didn't understand. And, as you know, Goodfellow is in the habit of collecting his overdue accounts with guns and knives, et cetera. So our high-society caper seems to be taking a seamy turn."

"Of course, Mitchell might be telling us all this to take our minds off them—him and Bruce Manley. They could easily have decided to go back and do the job, maybe for the money in the house, maybe to triple Bruce's inheritance."

"Well," Friedman said slowly, "that sounds a little heavy. I mean, Bruce may not be your typical bright-eyed kid-brother type, but I can't see him knocking off his own sister."

"Don't forget the possibility of drugs. And besides, Mitchell could've done the job himself. He'd profit indirectly."

"Maybe. Anyhow, I'm having a couple of selected junkies picked up. As soon as they start drying out, I'll offer them freedom in exchange for a little information on Goodfellow's recent transactions."

"Do you think Mitchell is a junkie?"

"If I had to guess, I'd say he's a beginning junkie. A skin-popper. I'll do a little research on that, too."

"What about Valenti? Was he a junkie?"

"No needle marks. It was all business with him, apparently. Karen wasn't a user either."

"How about Bruce Manley?"

"I'd guess he's dragging a little behind Mitchell. Brucie isn't as tough as he's led himself to believe. He's kind of chicken, in fact."

"I thought maybe Bruce and Billy were a love match. What d'you think?"

"I'd say it's an AC-DC situation."

"Have you been able to find out whether Bruce inherits Karen's estate?"

"No. Lawyers, as you know, just don't work that fast."

"Any word on the Volkswagen yet?"

"No, but— *Say,* I almost forgot. We got a make on those un-classified prints the lab found on the Drapers' outside garage door handle—the ones on top."

"Good. Who?"

"That kid. Dan Haywood. I just got the word from Markham."

I said slowly, "His father is a big-shot psychoanalyst—a guy who likes to really stir things up, I gather. If you can reach Markham, you'd better tell him to go slow." I paused, then added, "Tell him to check with me, on Haywood."

Friedman snorted ruefully. "The way these two cases are going, the whole Social Register seems to be— Oh, oh. Hold on a minute." The line clicked dead. Then: "My first two selected junkies have arrived. I'd better go. One of them is prime—a good buddy of Goodfellow's. The other's already halfway up the wall. Are you coming in, or what?"

I glanced at my watch: almost 5:30. "I don't think so. I still have to interview Walter Manley. Maybe I'll talk to Dan Haywood, too."

"Okay. I'm going to knock off about eight-thirty, I guess. We got some people coming over for Hanukkah week festivities. That's Jewish for Christmas. What're you doing for Christmas, by the way? Or, for that matter, what're you doing for Hanukkah?"

"I'll tell you later." I blinked, frowning at the phone. Then, changing the subject, I briefed Friedman on Jane Swanson. Five minutes later I was striding back to Rawlings' building. The sky was almost completely dark; a light winter rain had started to fall. Even the neighborhood's dingily curtained windows looked warm and dry.

An embossed card inscribed *Dwight Kellaway III* was thumbtacked to the door next to Dave Rawlings' apartment. I pressed Kellaway's buzzer, hopeful that Rawlings wouldn't hear. Almost immediately the door was opened by a tall, gangling young man in his middle twenties. His sparse sandy hair was raggedly cut just below the ear. He wore wire glasses, a tattered Beethoven sweat shirt, nondescript slacks and no shoes. His face was long and angular: lantern jaw, hollow cheeks and an elongated nose. His ginger eyebrows were full and bushy; his bright blue eyes were quick and clear. His mouth was wide and expressive—a hip Ichabod Crane.

I introduced myself, showed him the shield and asked to be let inside.

"Sure. Come on in. I haven't decided on a decorator yet. But I can offer you a packing box. Literally."

"That's fine."

He collapsed in an angular, loose-jointed posture on a mattress placed directly on the bare wooden floor. I sat, literally, on a box—a Haig and Haig box decorated with signs of the zodiac.

"I won't take much of your time, Mr. Kellaway," I began. "I just want a little information."

"Time I have, Lieutenant. Besides, I'm interested. I'm forty-three pages into the great American novel. For all I know, you could be page forty-four."

"What's your novel about?"

"It's about an intensely sensitive, intelligent young man who can't quite make it, despite all the so-called advantages. He can't make it in a succession of Ivy League colleges because he falls asleep in class. He can't make it in business because he snickers during sales meetings. He can't make it in hippieland because he can't take himself that seriously, plus he can't visualize himself growing turnips. And finally, he can't make it with girls, because"—he paused, then finished in a lower, more pensive voice—"because he wears glasses, I guess. I haven't figured that part out yet."

"Do you spend all your time writing?"

"No. I only write during the time I'd otherwise squander on double features or sex-starved girls. For money, I work at the post office. I'm in Out of State."

Because it was a relaxation, I bantered with him for another five minutes. Then I asked him whether he knew anything of his neighbors' movements during the previous night and early morning. He could only tell me that arriving home at one A.M., he saw their light on and "someone's shadow reflected on the gleaming man-made needles of their Woolworth's Yule tree."

"You say 'someone's shadow.' Do you mean one person, or two?"

"If I had to guess, Lieutenant, I'd say one. But it was just an impression. I was returning from the local all-night liquor store, where I'd just purchased a half gallon of cheap red wine, on which I planned to float effortlessly into page forty-four. My attention, naturally, was drawn to the glittering aluminum Christmas tree. And my recollection is that I saw a shadow—or shadows—inside. That's all." He spread his long arms. "Sorry."

"Are you acquainted with Mr. Rawlings and Miss Swanson?"

I was surprised to see his airy expression break up into a shy, confused, almost boyish blush. His eyes fell. His lashes, I saw, were surprisingly long.

"I know J—Miss Swanson," he mumbled, still avoiding my eyes. "But I don't know Rawlings very well."

I almost guffawed. She'd taken him to bed. She'd probably told him that she'd been overcome with girlish passion. I debated pursuing the point, deciding finally to let it go.

"What kind of a life do they have together, do you think?" I asked after a moment.

His good humor returned, along with his breezy poise. "Well, I'd say it isn't the world's most successful match, at least from Rawlings' point of view."

"How do you mean?"

"I mean simply that the poor guy's utterly, completely hung up on her, but she barely tolerates him. For which, I must say, I can't blame her. I don't understand how she could've got involved with him in the first place. He's one of those beetle-browed super males whose horizon is limited entirely by a woman in bed, a football game on TV and a car he can't afford in the garage."

"What kind of a car does he have?"

He shrugged indifferently. "Some kind of a super V-8, hydro hyped up, low slung, high-speed fire-engine red—a Pontiac, I think. I should know. He spends most of his time polishing it."

"What about Jane? What's she like?"

He glanced up sharply at my familiar use of the name. But when I didn't change expression, he frowned, thought about it, then said judiciously, "She's had a hard life. Sometimes she—comes over here, and we, ah, have a glass of wine. She needs someone to talk to. And after all—" He grinned. "I've got to get to page fifty somehow. Not to mention *three hundred* fifty."

"Has she told you much about herself?"

Again he frowned elaborately. "Over the months, quite a lot. It's not much of a story, I'm afraid. She was a good-looking teenager from Middle America. Her father took off when she was three, and her mother might just as well've taken off. Jane got married at seventeen, to get away from home. A year later she got divorced, or deserted—I forget which. Whereupon she started selling cigarettes and checking hats and hoofing—ending, naturally, in Las Vegas, the end of the hoofer's rainbow."

"How would you describe her personality?" I smiled. "After all, you're a forty-three-page novelist."

He ruefully returned the smile, almost shyly. Then, thinking about it, he said, "I suppose that Jane is just as one-dimensional as Rawlings. She's vain, self-centered and totally concerned with surface rather than substance—the traditional female vices. Still, when she has confidence in someone, she's not afraid to talk about herself, which takes a certain strength. She told me, for instance, about a man she met in Las Vegas. A European man, older than—" He broke off, eyes widening. Then: "Jesus Christ. That murder last night. She never told me his name, but—" He blinked, now tightly hugging his knees, staring incredulously at me. "Jesus. So that's it."

I got my hat, rising stiffly from the zodiac-decorated whiskey box. "You've been very helpful, Mr. Kellaway. I hope I'll see you again. Happy page forty-four."

13

I found Walter Manley in the same small sitting room his wife had occupied earlier in the day. Wearing a cashmere sweater and soft white sports shirt, he seemed perfectly cast as the affluent executive relaxing before dinner.

As the maid stepped aside, I saw Manley rise to his feet. His smile began as a suave, meaningless exercise in drawing-room etiquette, but ended a haunted, hollow-eyed failure. Gesturing me to a chair, he moved his arm in a short, uncertain arc, then slumped abruptly onto a brocaded love seat. On the elaborately carved side table I saw a half-finished highball, dark amber.

"Drink, Lieutenant?"

"No, thanks."

Frowning slightly, he nodded over my reply. His fingers twitched on the rich brocade; his gaze avoided mine.

I decided to sit quietly, watching him, waiting. Reacting normally, he should have immediately begun to press me for news of our investigation. His silence, then, could be revealing.

From a nearby room I heard a phone ring twice, followed by the hushed voice of the maid. Listening, Manley winced dully.

"I've been home all afternoon, except for—" He blinked. "Except for an hour at the funeral home. And that phone hasn't quit. Supposedly, they're all well-wishers. Actually, they're well-mannered ghouls, trying to participate vicariously in all this. It's the closest most of them get to living."

"I know. In my business they're occupational hazards. We call them the rubberneckers. They can't stand the sight of blood. But they can't stand not to look, either."

He toyed thoughtfully with his glass, then abruptly drained most of the remaining drink in one long gulp. With his chin uptilted, throat muscles sagging, he seemed suddenly vulnerable. I wondered how many highballs he'd had. His rigid, well-bred self-discipline, obviously second nature, made a sobriety assessment difficult. And shock could magnify liquor's impact. Guilt, too.

I drew a deep breath and leaned forward in my chair. It was time to go to work. "Mr. Manley," I began, "I'm sure you're familiar with our procedures. Contrary to popular opinion, we don't usually come up with many inspired solutions to a murder. We just collect all the facts we can—all the tips, all the gossip, all the little bits of unrelated information. Everything. Then we try to fit it all together. We look for tie-ins, points of intersection. When we finally find our man—the murderer—we discover, naturally, that ninety-five percent of our effort has been totally wasted. For instance—" I paused, assessing his reaction. He offered no response; his manner was aloof, indifferent, as if he were politely half-listening to a completely predictable profit-and-loss recitation. I watched him absently arranging his shirt collar. He was one of those men who wore clothes beautifully. Meaning that he constantly made almost imperceptible body-adjustments, subtly accommodating himself to the line of his clothing. But he was beyond conscious posing, beyond vanity. His self-confident presence and his iron-gray good looks were inherited, not acquired.

"For instance," I continued, "we've learned that your son Bruce was with Karen last evening. So, naturally, we're checking on his movements. We don't seriously think he could have committed the murder. Psychologically I'd say it's almost impossible. Still"—I shrugged—"still, he had the opportunity, and he had a possible motive. So—"

"Motive?" He was frowning. But he seemed merely puzzled—as if the profit-and-loss recital had taken a mildly distressing turn.

"Yes, Mr. Manley. We've been checking with your lawyers, at your wife's suggestion. And we've discovered that Bruce inherits Karen's own inheritance."

"But—" Incredulous, he was getting his strikingly blue eyes into focus. "But that's preposterous." His voice had deepened, became more authoritative.

"I agree. As I said. Still"—I spread my hands—"we have to check everything out. As a matter of fact—" I leaned back, pretending a casual detachment, pitching my voice to an offhand note as I said, "As a matter of fact, I've got to check you out—ask you to account for your movements last night."

"You're joking." His voice was flat, for the first time accented with the offhand, understated arrogance of the stereotyped upper class.

"No," I answered slowly, "I'm not joking. Unfortunately."

"Are you telling me," he said, "that you think I had a motive for killing my own daughter?" As he spoke, his body tightened visibly, became wrathfully rigid.

"I'm telling you that we have a statement from a qualified witness which states that you were involved with a woman known to"—I hesitated, choosing the words—"to travel in the same circle as Valenti and your daughter."

"Your 'witness' is a liar, Lieutenant. And you're repeating a libelous story." Banging his glass down hard on the exquisitely carved table, he rose to his feet and crossed to the doorway in three long, angry strides. Closing the door, turning, stepping a single pace toward me, he stood in the center of the small room. His fists were clenched at his sides; his eyes bulged with barely suppressed belligerence. His wide, handsomely molded mouth was tightly compressed. His voice was very low, very intimidating as he said, "If my wife should hear you, the consequences could be unpleasant."

I rose to face him. Dropping my voice to a flat, official monotone, locking my eyes with his, I replied, "I'll give you the complete story as it was presented to me, Mr. Manley. When you've heard it, you can either confirm or deny it. That's all I'm asking: just a confirmation or a denial. Fair?"

His reply was a short, contemptuous snort. But his eyes were watchful.

"My information is that you've often been seen with a girl named Candice Weiss. I also understand that your, ah, friendship with Miss Weiss was known to both your daughter and Valenti." I paused. Then, pitching my voice to a slower, graver cadence, I said, "Now, is that a true statement or a false statement?"

Drawing a deep breath, loudly exhaling, he stood squarely before me, regarding me with a kind of exasperated impatience, as if he'd regretfully decided to discipline me for some infraction of executive fiat.

"I've only one thing to say to you, Lieutenant. And that's this—" Again he drew a deep breath, making an elaborate effort to control himself. "It's true, I know a girl named Candice Weiss. I keep two horses in Golden Gate Park. Mrs. Weiss—she's divorced—keeps a horse at the same stable. She may have known Karen; I really couldn't say. She may also have known Valenti. She probably did, in fact, if she knew Karen. Now—" He hesitated elaborately. "Now, that's all I'm going to say on the subject. Furthermore, if you intend to pursue this—this ridiculous tactic any further, I'll be compelled to call my lawyers and let them deal with you. And I should warn you that my lawyers are very well paid. Which means that they're accustomed to getting results, no matter who gets hurt in the process."

For a long, quiet moment I studied him, hopeful that he'd drop his eyes. When he didn't, I nodded slowly, attempting to project a resigned, reluctant regret. Drawing a plastic card from my pocket, I read him his rights in flat officialese.

"Please contact your lawyer and be downtown within an hour, Mr. Manley," I concluded, turning abruptly toward the door. I allowed my shoulders to slump, as if the necessity for dealing with Manley as a suspect distressed me.

He let me reach the door, with my hand on the knob.

"Lieutenant."

Turning, I saw him sink down on the brocaded sofa, suddenly round-shouldered, plainly dejected, once more hollow-eyed. He looked like a washed-up actor who couldn't remember his lines—a caricature of success, no longer its urbane embodiment. His fingers were again fretfully picking at the sofa's fabric.

"If it weren't for Denise—my wife—I wouldn't give a damn," he said dully. "But she just can't take any more. Not now. The lawyers can protect me. But they can't help Denise."

With an obvious effort, he raised his eyes, sighing raggedly. "My only recourse is to approach you as a—a gentleman."

The phrase struck such an odd, archaic note that, caught by surprise, I almost guffawed. Plainly, he had little hope for his one-gentleman-to-another appeal.

"Tell me about it, Mr. Manley," I said quietly. "I'll do the best I can for you."

Averting his eyes, speaking in a low, rapid monotone, he said, "There's nothing especially unusual about my—friendship with Candice. My wife and I, like many of the people we know, lead very complex lives—very civilized lives—with no unpleasant surprises. Two or three days pass, and we don't see each other for more than an hour or two. We eat breakfast separately, and we have separate bedrooms. When we have dinner together, it's usually with someone else—an occasion of some sort. Everything is carefully planned. It's an intricate game, played according to a rather elaborate set of rules. And the rules specify that nothing either of us does, ah, extracurricularly can interfere with our public life—our images, if you will. We haven't missed an important party—a benefit, or a museum opening —in years. In public, we're always seen together. We always smile. What's more, in public, we enjoy each other's company. Even in private, we never fight. At some point, probably a long while ago, we lost both the capacity to love and to hate. So we smile, politely, both for our friends and our servants. Beyond that—" He listlessly lifted both hands a few inches above the sofa, palms up, then allowed them to fall back. "Beyond that, there's not much. We use the maid as a—a kind of message center. And the—the governess, too, when the children were smaller." As he finished, he raised his eyes almost furtively, as if he'd committed a small social sin.

"Did Valenti know of your affair with Mrs. Weiss?"

"Yes."

"Was he trying to blackmail you?"

"Not directly. He was too—too goddamn suave for that. It would have shocked his gigolo's sensibilities to ask for money directly."

"Indirectly, then."

"Yes. Indirectly."

"How?"

"He'd set up a so-called import-export business. And it seemed as if he was always in need of 'venture capital,' as he called it."

"How much 'venture capital' have you supplied in the past six months?"

"About twelve thousand. Not an enormous sum."

"Substantial, though."

He shrugged. "It's all relative, Lieutenant. I'm a wealthy man. And Valenti's little scheme at least had the virtue of allowing me a tax write-off."

"According to the rules your wife and you live by, though—by your own statement—there isn't much that Valenti could've done that would've really hurt you."

"Maybe." It was an exhausted rejoinder.

"You just implied, though," I pressed him, "that you don't stand in each other's way, so far as extramarital affairs are concerned."

"True. But the agreement is entirely tacit. That's the key word in these arrangements. The other party can *suspect* anything, and probably does. But he—or she—must never actually *know*. It gets back to face-saving—as so much really does, I'm discovering. Besides," he said wryly, "there's always the vultures who stalk the privileged classes, euphemistically called divorce lawyers. A wife with a solid case of proven adultery can find both freedom and financial security for life. Not to mention the lawyer; he's always the winner. There's also the temptation for a preemptive strike: if one party has a clear advantage, he's wise to take it. The next year matters could be reversed. And besides all those very practical considerations, there's the fact that I've lived thirty years with my wife. For a few of those years I loved her. I'm still fond of her. So for those reasons, I don't want to see her humiliated. Not now. It—it's morally unfair. It's also impolite." He paused, his eyes reflective, sad. "Unhappily," he said softly, "a breach of etiquette seems more reprehensible than a violation of morality."

For a moment, watching him, I was silently, helplessly entrapped in the memories his cynical, dead-voiced recital had evoked. Pulling myself back, I asked him for an account of his movements on Monday night.

He smiled ruefully. "My wife spent Sunday and Monday with friends in the Napa Valley, and didn't return home until about eleven P.M. on Monday. She was ducking out on the pre-Christmas party rounds, which is currently a very chic thing to do. I had business—bona-fide business—in Los Angeles on Monday morning. I flew down to Los Angeles on Sunday night and returned Monday afternoon. I had a quiet dinner at Candice's apartment. I gave her a Christmas present. I returned home about midnight. My wife was already in bed, and her light was out, signaling that I wasn't to enter. So I got a drink and went to bed. I read for a half-hour, then went to sleep."

"Was anyone in the house except you and your wife?"

He seemed to pity the transparency of the question. His manner was disdainful, almost condescending as he said, "It was the help's night off. I don't have an alibi, Lieutenant. And my wife is a sound sleeper."

"What kind of cars do you have?"

"I have a Continental. My wife has a Mercedes."

"Do you have any objection to our lab technicians checking over your cars?"

"Not really." As he said it, he seemed suddenly to slump, exhausted. He was staring at the same view that had so transfixed his wife earlier in the day. The Golden Gate Bridge was traced in long, graceful arcs of tiny yellow lights; the scattered houses in the Marin County hills were diamond chips strewn carelessly across the darkness. Moonlight fell in a straight silver pathway across the black water of the bay.

I rose to my feet. "I'll be in touch with you, Mr. Manley.

I'd like to have you notify me, personally, before you leave the city."

He inclined his handsome head politely, murmuring something inaudible, still staring out at his expensive view.

14

I treated myself to a rack of lamb at the Loft, a small, casually elegant Union Street restaurant just four blocks from my apartment —and three blocks from the Haywoods' flat. Even though it was a weekday night, the dining room was crowded. I ate slowly, watching the diners, listening to the laugh-rippled murmur of their conversation. I could sense their mood of holiday excitement. Saturday was Christmas. "Only three shopping days before Christmas," the papers were proclaiming. It was a depressing statistic, evoking bitterly twisted memories of happier days. I'd done my Christmas shopping in less than an hour, buying a book for Darrell and a record album for Claudia. So far, I hadn't received a package from either of them.

I finished the lamb, then the last of the salad. A half cup of coffee remained. I would sit for a few relaxed minutes, sipping the coffee, watching the diners' faces, listening to random snatches of their conversation. Then I would call on the Haywoods—not because I should, but, somehow, because I must.

Three days left—

Last year Darrell and Claudia had flown out from Detroit to spend Christmas with me. Claudia had slept in the single bedroom, Darrell and I together in the living-room hideabed. Gaily, Claudia had undertaken to cook Christmas dinner—a disaster. They'd spoken vaguely of staying through New Year's, using my car for side trips, hopefully with other teenagers. But among my few friends, only the Friedmans had teenage children, both of them slightly younger than Darrell and Claudia, therefore unacceptable.

On Christmas Day, with Kreiger out of town and Friedman ill, I'd been called for work at four P.M., supervising two separate homicides, both the result of holiday drinking, aggravating holiday depression. On the twenty-sixth, I'd caught three hours' sleep in my office. So my children had gone back to Detroit on the twenty-seventh, smiling gravely as they boarded the plane.

I finished the last sip of coffee and dropped a five-dollar bill on the waiter's tray. Suddenly I wanted to be out in the wet, anonymous night, working.

The Haywoods' porch light was lit, and as I pressed the buzzer I immediately heard footsteps hurriedly approaching. Even with the night chain on, I could recognize fear frozen in her face as she peeked out at me. When she opened the door, fumbling, she stood rigid, one hand pressed flat to her stomach, the other hand tightly gripping the doorknob. Her eyes were vague. Her mouth was open, as if she were gasping for breath.

"He's gone," she whispered. "He's not here."

"Where is he?"

"I—I'm not sure. Bobby, my youngest, is staying overnight with friends in Marin County. I—I drove him over, about three-thirty this afternoon. Dan stayed here, listening to records. He—he seemed morose. Depressed. I asked him if anything was wrong. He said no, there wasn't. I wanted him to come with us, but he wouldn't. I—I told him I'd be home by six-thirty or seven, to fix dinner. We were going to have steaks. But—" Her voice trailed off; her eyes wandered beyond me, as if she hoped to see her oldest son somewhere in the darkness.

I stepped forward, taking her arm. Even though she moved woodenly beside me, the touch was exciting.

"Let's go inside. Tell me about it. I'll make some calls. I don't think there's anything to worry about."

But neither of us, I knew, believed it.

We were in the living room, sitting as we had yesterday. I leaned toward her, saying again, "Tell me about it."

She held her hands tightly clasped in her lap, as she had the day before—her prim, proper finishing-school posture.

"I can't tell you anything more." Her voice was unsteady; her eyes glistened. She was shaking her head in slow, helpless bafflement. "I've told you everything."

"Have you contacted his father?"

"I tried. But he wasn't at home. Or at the office, either."

"Does he live close by?"

"Ten or twelve blocks away."

"Did Dan say anything after I left last night—anything about Sunday? Anything at all?"

She began to shake her head dully, then interrupted the movement, dropping her head, frowning.

"What did he say?" I pressed her. "It's important for you to tell me everything, even if it seems trivial."

Lifting her eyes with obvious effort, she said, "The only thing he said—concerned you, I'm afraid."

"What was it?"

"He said—" She paused. Then, drawing a deep breath and again dropping her eyes: "He said that you were—interested in me. That you were 'making a big deal of everything' because of your interest in me." Her mouth moved in a brief, exhausted smile.

Feeling myself flush, I realized that I was snorting derisively, confused. "He's probably down at headquarters, then," I said quickly, "reporting me for unofficerlike conduct."

She managed another small, shadowed smile. But she was treading the ragged edge.

"Besides," I said, "I don't even know your first name. Which, incidentally, I should—for my official departmental interrogation report."

"It's Ann."

"Ann," I repeated. "Good. Thanks."

I allowed a moment to pass, then: "He must've said something else. You talked yesterday, didn't you? You *must've* talked after I left."

"We didn't talk much, I'm afraid. Dan seemed very—resentful. Very hostile." She paused thoughtfully. Then she said, "He did say something about not 'taking a fall' for one silly prank. Which, I assumed, referred to his difficulty on the streetcar—I told you about that yesterday."

"You say you 'assumed' that's what it was about. But did he mention that streetcar incident particularly? Or were you just taking it for granted?"

"Well—" She looked down at her clasped fingers.

"Did he use the word 'prank'? Or is that your word?"

Hopelessly she shook her head. "I—I'm not sure, Lieutenant. I just can't seem to think. Right now, I feel as if I'd like to just—just lie down and go to sleep, and not wake up again until the whole world's completely different."

I got to my feet, standing over her. "Everyone, I suppose, feels like that once in a while. I've often thought that the animals have the right idea: hibernation. Just sleep through the winter. In the spring, everything looks better."

"Different, anyhow."

I smiled down at her, asking, "Where's your phone?"

"In the—"

A key rattled in the door. She was on her feet, close beside me, facing the hallway. I heard footsteps. Dan Haywood was standing in the archway. He was wearing the same sweater he'd worn yesterday, and the same khaki pants. A tall, dark-haired man with pale, intense eyes and a hard, precise mouth brushed past the boy. The man wore a dark tweed suit, expensively cut. His face was masklike: rigid and unrevealing—a face calculated to disguise emotion, never reveal it. He carried himself with calm, arrogant authority.

"Who're you?" he asked, facing me at a distance of three feet. His voice was low, vibrant with hostility, edged with a quiet, controlled scorn.

"That's Lieutenant Hastings," the boy said, from the archway. "He's the head man. I told you about him."

The man stood very erect, fingers flexing at his sides. Briefly it occurred to me that he looked as if he were posing for a heroic statue. He drew a deep breath, deliberately looking me over. Watching him, I realized that he, like myself, was a professional inquisitor—an expert at intimidation and persuasion. At will, he could seem either a distant friend or a dangerous enemy. He could be brutal or solicitous —a cold, subtle practitioner who could deftly play the subconscious against the conscious, fear against hope, friendship against loneliness and despair.

"I am Arthur Haywood," he said slowly, holding my gaze with his inexorable gray eyes. "Dan's father."

I nodded acknowledgment, determined to remain silent as long as possible. Not knowing whether the boy had been questioned about the fingerprint, I was at a disadvantage. Belatedly, I realized ruefully that instead of leisurely enjoying rack of lamb, I should have been putting out a call for Markham. It was a mistake that could cost me dearly during the next few minutes. If Markham had given the boy a hard time interrogating him on the premises, without parental consent, I could have a problem.

"Are you aware," Haywood was saying, "that your men have been harassing my son?"

I settled myself more firmly, crossing my arms. If he was angry, and I remained calm, I could still take the first round.

"*Are* you?"

"You'll have to explain what you mean by 'harassing,' Mr. Haywood."

"I mean, precisely, that one of your men entered this house today and tried to intimidate Dan. Entry was effected illegally. Dan wasn't advised of his rights under the Constitution. Furthermore, as a minor, he is entitled to special protection from police harassment."

"As a matter of fact," I said slowly, "I was just about to phone downtown, when you came in. Mrs. Haywood, naturally, was very upset, coming home to find the boy gone. I was going to try to ease her mind, if I could." I glanced first at her pale, drawn face, then at the boy, who shifted slightly, dropping his eyes.

"If she'd been here, as she was supposed to be, the boy

wouldn't've had to find me—interrupt me with patients, in fact."
Haywood's tone was unchanged—calculatedly brutal, insulting. He
didn't bother to look at the woman.

"Would you like to wait for me to call my office?" I asked.
"When I do, maybe I can give you some answers."

"You needn't bother. I'm leaving here for my lawyer's. You can
talk to him. But in the meantime—" Haywood glanced briefly at his
watch, then raised a threatening forefinger. "In the meantime, Lieutenant, I warn you: any further harassment of Dan will cost you
dearly. I'm not going to go into the details of my standing in the
community; if you're interested, my—Mrs. Haywood can fill you in.
I promise you, though, that you'll pay, personally, for any more of
these police-state tactics." He held me with his pale, arrogant eyes
while he slowly lowered the warning forefinger. His timing was perfect.

I would have been wise to simply lower my gaze, refusing to
answer, waiting for him to leave. But his cold contempt suddenly
seemed too plainly a distillate of the constant street-corner scorn no
cop can ever quite forget.

I withdrew my billfold and took out a business card. Handing
the card to him, I said, "I try to be in the office most mornings, Mr.
Haywood. If you'd like to call ahead, I can probably make time for
you."

I had my brief, spurious moment of victory: a plain flicker of
naked, uncontrolled rage smoldered briefly deep behind his eyes.

"It's *Doctor* Haywood," he said very softly, "not 'Mister.' And
if I were you, I'd—" He interrupted his own banality, saving himself
from even a small defeat. Then, drawing a slow, deep breath, he
elaborately checked the time. Turning to Ann Haywood, he ac-
knowledged her presence for the first time, saying, "My lawyer will
be in touch with you first thing tomorrow—possibly tonight. In the
meantime—" He inclined his head an inch toward me. "In the meantime, I'd advise you to invite your—friend to leave. But in any case,
he's expressly forbidden to interrogate Dan."

Arthur Haywood turned away abruptly. He paused a moment
in the archway, shaking hands with the boy, crisply repeating his

parting instructions in a clear, concise voice. Then, without looking back, he was gone.

As the front door closed, I held Dan's eyes. For the briefest moment I thought he would speak—asking, not demanding. But in the next moment he'd disappeared down the hallway. I heard his rapid footsteps, then the slam of a door.

As I turned to Ann Haywood, I saw her sigh once, very deeply. She stood staring at the empty archway. She held both hands clasped, knuckle-white, just at her waist.

Then she sobbed, suddenly, quickly twisting away, sinking down on the sofa. She held both hands in a symmetrical temple just in front of her face, fingertips tight against the bridge of her nose. Still turned away, she was struggling for self-control, testing herself with repeated sighs. Finally: "I—I'm sorry, Lieutenant. I—" She sniffled.

"Do you want a handkerchief?"

"Yes, thank you. I—I never seem to have one when I need it."

I passed her my handkerchief, sitting to face her, watching her dab at her eyes.

"You can blow your nose," I said. "Keep it. I'll charge the department."

Tremulously she smiled, then obeyed. "I'll—" She gulped. "I'll launder it for you."

"Fine."

As she worked at her face, her snuffling slowly subsided. "I'm afraid Arthur doesn't think much of me as a mother figure," she said finally.

"It's none of my official business, but I don't think much of him as a father figure."

She hesitated, then said in a small, chastened voice, "Arthur has very high standards—for himself, and everyone else. Unfortunately, he usually manages to meet his own standards."

"High standards can be tough on a kid."

"On everyone else, too, I'm afraid."

"I suppose so."

We sat silently for a long, uncomfortable moment, avoiding each other's eyes.

"What's happening, Lieutenant? What's happening to Dan? Is there evidence against him—something my husband suspects?"

"I can't answer that. Not until I've talked to my men, then talked to Dan. I've been working on another case for most of the day. Your hus—Mr. Haywood had me at a disadvantage. Which, luckily, he didn't seem to fully realize."

She smiled very faintly. "It's 'Doctor.' Not 'Mister.' "

I absently answered her smile. I was rethinking Arthur Haywood's threats, and trying to assess Dan's reactions. I was thinking, too, that if Markham had actually harassed the boy, there wasn't much I could do to make matters officially worse. If the department was already in trouble, a gamble might be the best gambit—like Friedman's car heist.

"I have a very unorthodox proposition for you," I said thoughtfully.

Her eyes lightened, ruefully quizzical. "A proposition, Lieutenant?"

"Yes. I'd like you to visit the neighbors for a half-hour or so. I'd like to talk to your son, without you in the house. After I've talked to him, I should be able to tell you something about the case. I can't promise good news. But at least it might be something."

"You say *should* be able to tell me something."

"That's the best I can do. There's no point in making a promise I can't keep."

"If my husband finds out—and he will—we'll both suffer for it."

"Maybe."

Her hands were in her lap, tightly clasped. Staring down at her fingers, she said, "I—I can't think of any neighbors that I can just pop in on at this time of the night."

"Go to the Loft. Have a drink. When I'm finished, I'll come for you. That might be better, in fact."

With frightened eyes she searched my face. Then, plainly without hope, she agreed.

15

I tapped softly on Dan Haywood's bedroom door. Entering on his muttered invitation, I saw him sitting hunched at a small desk. Turning, seeing me, his eyes widened.

"Wh—" He craned his neck, looking behind me.

"Your mother is out." I closed the door and sat on the bed to face him. "I want to talk to you."

"But my—my father. He'll—"

"He won't do anything to me, Dan. And he won't do anything to you, either. Not if you tell me the truth. That's the only way to straighten this out: tell the truth."

"I *have* been telling the truth." His voice was dogged, sullen. He was obviously trying to achieve the same loose, slack-shouldered insolence with which he'd confronted me yesterday.

"Inspector Markham talked to you today." It was a statement, not a question.

He didn't reply.

"He told you that we have evidence you were on the Draper premises Sunday night."

"Listen, my father will—"

"What were you doing at the Drapers' garage?"

"What makes you think I was at their stupid—" He seemed

baffled. His eyes circled the room, as though searching for some way to escape.

"Your fingerprints are on the door handle," I said quietly.

"Prove it." His voice slipped to a momentary falsetto as he spat out his challenge from childhood.

In spite of myself, I smiled slightly. "I *can* prove it, Dan. Take my word for it."

"You're just going along with that other one. Markham. Running the same crappy bluff." He seemed to find assurance in his own defiance. He rose, staring down at me—again the insolent, overprivileged young rebel. "I'm going to call my father. Where's my mother, anyhow?"

"Out." I got to my feet, facing him squarely.

His lip curled. "Christ, that's really something. She's *in* with you—going along with you."

For a moment I didn't answer. Then, slowly, I said, "From your tone, you don't seem to think much of your mother."

"Not when she pulls crap like this."

I allowed another long moment to pass, looking steadily at him. I realized that I might be about to make my second mistake of the evening.

"My boy is a little younger than you are," I said quietly. "He doesn't live with me. If I see him once a year, I'm lucky. But I'll tell you something—" I drew a slow breath, moving a half-step toward him. "If my son ever talked about his mother like that—in the same tone you've just used—I think I'd probably belt him across the room. Before I thought about it—before I could stop myself. And I'm in the business of not belting people, believe it or not. I'm in the business of always—*always*—thinking before I put a hand on anyone."

His reaction was strangely subdued. We stood very close, subtly, secretly suspended together, staring at each other. His lips parted, uncertainly. He looked as if he was about to say something conciliatory. But then the mouth hardened; his face contracted, again defiant. "I've seen the cops," he muttered. "I've seen how long they think about it before they start swinging."

"I'm talking about me, Dan. Me, personally. And I'm talking about you. Personally. This is a private conversation. Me and you."

His response was a skeptical snort, a shifting of his feet, a restless realignment of his careless slouch.

"Your mother," I said, "is just about sick with worry."

He started to shrug. Then, eying me warily, he exhaled loudly, again shifting his feet, now thrusting his hands deep in his pockets.

"Just tell me what you were doing in the Draper garage, Dan. Tell me the truth. That's all I'm after."

"I wasn't *in* the goddamn garage. I—Christ—" He tried to edge around me, making for the door. I moved with him.

"Your fingerprints were *over* Mrs. Draper's prints. That's fact, Dan. You turned that handle after she did. We can produce incontrovertible expert testimony to that effect. And you know it, just as well as I do."

"What d'you mean, 'expert testimony'?"

"I mean that in court a fingerprint expert would—"

"In *court?*"

Suddenly, behind his eyes, I could see the fear inside him. I paused, silently watching him. Then, pitching my voice to a note of quiet concern, I said, "We've got a woman murdered, Dan. We've got you at the scene. First we had you across the street—by your own statement, nothing more than a witness, giving us some unsubstantiated information about a black man that no one else saw. Now, though, we get a little surprise: we discover that you were on the Draper premises at the time of the murder. We—"

"Murder." His voice was hushed now. "You think I murdered her."

I didn't answer, watching him squirm. Then: "Did Inspector Markham take the clothes you were wearing Sunday night?"

"Wh—why d'you—"

"*Did* he?"

"Yes."

"The shoes, too?"

He nodded. Then, attempting a cynical bravado, he said, "He gave me a receipt. D'you want to see it?"

I shook my head, saying, "If we should find blood on those clothes, Dan, you'll be in trouble. You realize that, don't you?"

"You won't find any blood."

"You can't wash it away, you know. It's impossible. And a microscopic spot is all we need to—"

He lunged for the door. I was behind him before he'd reached the knob. I slammed him flat against the door, splitting the panel with his forehead. With my forearm braced against the back of his neck, I kicked at his legs, then found a hammerlock with my free hand.

"Go limp." I jerked at his twisted arm, feeling him rise to his toes in pain. "Go limp, or I'll handcuff you and call for a squad car. The whole neighborhood'll see you hauled away."

Slowly his muscular young body slackened. Then he fell back against me, panting noisily. I felt his body suddenly convulse, and heard him sob. Cautiously I worked him back toward the bed, then released him. He slumped down on the edge of the bed, head lowered, wiping at his eyes.

"I don't know why I did it," he said indistinctly. "I don't know why the hell I did it. Such a—a goddamn silly thing. And now I— you—" He began to shake his head, hopelessly.

Thinking of Ann Haywood, I felt a cold, empty sense of regret as I sat on the bed beside him, far enough away to give myself room if he came for me.

"You were teed off at Cindy Wallace," I said softly. "That's how it started, didn't it? She put you off—gave you a hard time."

He nodded, still wiping at his eyes.

"You sat in your car after Cindy went inside."

Again he nodded. He was no longer sobbing, but simply sat staring down at the floor, his limp hands hanging down between his thighs. "It was so—so goddamn stupid. I—I—" He began again to shake his head. "So stupid."

"Tell me about it, Dan. If I can help you, I will."

"There—there isn't anything to tell. Not—not really. I was just sitting there, smoking a cigarette. Steaming, really steaming. And I saw this—" He gulped. But now he'd started, and I knew he'd keep on with it. "I saw this broad drive up. Mrs. Draper. I'd seen her once or twice; I knew who she was. So I—I watched her stop in front of the garage, with the headlights on, while she opened the door. It—it didn't take her very long. But it was long enough for me to see that goddamn—" He broke off, shaking his head; then, doggedly: "That goddamn leopard head, on the wall of the garage. So then she drove inside and closed the door behind her. And I—I sat there, feeling like I was going to—to pop, or something, the way you do sometimes. I guess if someone my age had come along, I'd've picked a fight with him. I've done that. Plenty of times. But Sunday, there was just this —this goddamn leopard head. And pretty soon all I could think about was getting it—getting inside that garage and taking the head and splitting. Just"—he shrugged—"just for the hell of it." Again he shrugged, vaguely shaking his head. His eyes were empty.

"What happened next?" I asked quietly.

"So then, the next thing I knew, the door was opening again. She was coming back out on the street, and closing the door behind her, and walking around to the front door. And—" He sighed.

"And you got out of the car," I prompted him.

"What?" He was frowning, puzzled.

"You got out of the car."

"No. Not then."

"All right," I said, unwilling to break into his mood. "Go ahead. I'm sorry."

"Well, she just—just turned into the tunnel entrance, and disappeared behind all those plants. I waited a couple of minutes, to be sure she was inside. Five minutes, maybe. I finished my cigarette, I remember. And then I—"

"Did you actually see her enter the front door—unlock it?"

He shook his head. "The angle was wrong. I just saw her for a second, once she left the sidewalk. Like I say, the plants hid her."

"All right. What happened then?"

"Well, then, I—" He sighed raggedly. "Then I got out of my car, and walked across the street and tried the garage door. It—it was locked. I jiggled it a couple of times, and gave it a good pull. But when it didn't give, I got back in the car. I was just about to drive away, when I saw the goddamn garage door open. So I—"

"You saw it open from the inside. Is that it?"

He nodded. "It kind of went up by itself. I thought maybe they had an opener. I figured that they'd heard me. So I just—just took off."

"No one came out."

"No. Like I say, I thought it was run by an opener. Then I realized that someone might be inside, looking for me. So I split. Drove off."

His face was slack; his mouth was twitching, distorted by misery and uncertainty. His eyes were wide, vulnerable.

Was he acting?

I allowed the silence to continue. Finally, when he began to shift uneasily, I said, "This leopard head. What were you going to do with it?"

He moved his shoulders listlessly. "Bring it home." He waved his hand around the room. Following the gesture, I saw a random collection of contraband: street signs, hub caps, posters, even concrete garden statuary. "I don't know why," he was saying, "but it seemed like, then, I just—just had to have that leopard head."

I sat silently for another half-minute. Then I said, "If what you're saying is true, I wish you'd kindly explain why the hell you didn't tell me this yesterday."

"I—I don't know. It just seemed like, you being a cop, I—"

I watched my fist flexing, resting on my knee. "That's beautiful," I said finally. "Because I'm a cop, you do your best to screw up a homicide investigation. What about the black man? Was he part of your little romp?"

"Yes."

"He didn't exist."

"No."

"Did you tell Inspector Markham any of this when he interrogated you today—anything about Mrs. Draper, or the leopard head, or the fictitious black man?"

"No."

"Why not?"

"Because he—he came on pretty strong. Like you did, right

now. He said that, at the least, you guys had me for giving false evidence, or impeding justice, or something, just because you could place me at the scene, and I hadn't told you I was there. He said I could get five years, or something, just for that—just for lying. Then he started in on the black man. And so I just—" He slowly raised his hands, palms up, then let them fall down between his thighs, hanging loosely.

I glanced at my watch. She'd been sitting in the Loft for almost an hour. I took him through his story again, cross-questioning him. Exhausted, he was fully cooperative. His story didn't change. I told him that if his story checked, he had nothing to worry about. Then, after using my radio to call in for a crime lab pickup of the Haywood car, I walked to the Loft. The rain was falling with a steady, monotonous, all-night rhythm.

16

I walked slowly toward the Loft, shoulders hunched inside my raincoat. At the restaurant, before I met Ann Haywood, I must call the office.

But what would I say?

What orders would I give?

If Dan Haywood's story was true, Draper should be picked up, taken downtown, interrogated. His premises should be searched, his clothing examined for bloodstains. The house had been under constant surveillance since he'd reported the crime. Therefore, if Draper had killed his wife, then her billfold was probably hidden somewhere in the house, along with the weapon and Draper's bloodstained clothing.

If the boy's story was true.

The time was almost ten-thirty. Draper and his small daughter could be asleep. Certainly the girl would be asleep. It would be necessary, then, to wake her, get her dressed and take her to the Youth Guidance Center, while her father was being detained for questioning and the house searched. If we arrested Draper on a charge of murder, the girl would remain at the Center until her father was arraigned. Then a judge would dispose of her case, probably sending her to grandparents, pending trial.

Tomorrow her mother was being buried.

Tomorrow her father could be under arrest.

If Dan Haywood's story was true.

I turned the last corner; ahead was the Loft. I realized that my steps were lagging. I had a decision to make, orders to issue, acting on Dan's new information. But I felt a sense of reluctance. It would be easier—safer—to delay the orders until tomorrow, leaving the final decision to Kreiger. He'd once said that a captain's job was to sit in a warm office, safe from sad, accusing eyes, and make the tough decisions.

At the Loft's doorway, sheltered from the rain, I stood perfectly still, thoughtfully looking down at my shoes.

Mothers and fathers—sons and daughters. The Manleys. The Drapers. From each family, one was dead. In each family, one was suspected.

It was a grisly, utterly predictable truism of police work that if a man is murdered, you must first question his wife. Then his father. Next his brother and finally his mistress. Most homicide victims, at some time in their lives, had once loved their eventual murderer.

I stepped inside the Loft's small lobby and dialed the pay phone, calling the office. Canelli was just going off duty. Markham had checked out without having written a report on his interrogation of Dan Haywood. Assuming he'd finished the interrogation about five P.M., Markham wasn't at fault. Like the rest of us, he'd been working sixteen hours a day.

I told Canelli to verify the Draper surveillance, then asked him to meet me at the Draper residence in about an hour. Cheerfully, he agreed. As I hung up, he was beginning a long preamble concerning possible new evidence in the Manley case. I asked him to save it, thanking him for his uncomplaining cooperation.

Ann Haywood was sitting at the far end of the bar. With her London-style gabardine raincoat, scuffed loafers and a kerchief tied over her blond, bedraggled hair, she seemed especially woebegone, out of place in the casually posh bar.

She turned quickly as I sat beside her. Wordlessly, she looked at me. In a few sentences I told her that if her son had told me the truth, neither of them had anything to worry about. To her urgent, un-spoken question, I answered that yes, I believed Dan had told me the truth—that he was guilty of erratic, antisocial behavior, but nothing more.

Seeing that her glass was empty, I asked her if she wanted an-other drink.

"I—I'd better get back."

"A drink might help. Plus, it might be a good idea to give Dan a little time to think things over."

"Well—" She hesitated. "If it's a quick drink."

I ordered a bourbon and water for her and a 7-Up for myself, automatically explaining that hard liquor didn't agree with me, half apologizing. Uncertainly smiling in response, she nervously tucked at her lank hair. Watching her, I was remembering Arthur Haywood's icy contempt as he instructed her concerning their son.

Yet once they'd loved each other. They'd joined their bodies, produced children, watched the children grow. Now they hated each other. And the son, Dan, was punishing them by punishing himself.

As if to mirror my thoughts, she said quietly, "I've made a mess of things, with Dan. I—guess it's pretty obvious."

"Don't blame yourself. From what I saw, your ex-husband de-serves at least half the blame. Maybe a lot more."

"That's so easy, though: just blame the other person."

"He's blaming you. In public. I can imagine what he does in private."

"*Did* in private," she corrected. "We don't really communicate, I'm afraid. Maybe we never did." She bit her lip, stared solemnly ahead for a moment, then drank a third of her highball in two long gulps. Placing the glass gravely on the bar, she said, "You're really very—kind. I want to thank you."

"I told you yesterday: I've been through it myself. A divorce, I mean."

"Do you have children?"

"Yes. A boy and a girl. Teenagers. They live in Detroit, with their mother."

She hesitated. Then she asked, "How is it that you live here? I mean—" She didn't finish it.

Avoiding her eyes, I sipped at the 7-Up. Then I said, "I was born here. My mother lives in San Rafael. It seemed the logical place to come."

She didn't reply. I realized that my reluctance to answer her question fully would close the door she'd tentatively opened. So I said, "Until I got married, I spent most of my time playing football and reading my clippings, which were beginning to get older and fewer every year. I met my wife when I was playing for the Detroit Lions. I was twenty-five; she was a little younger. She—" I looked at Ann Haywood, then away, clearing my throat and frowning slightly. "She was a little like you, as a matter of fact. She was blond, and— wonderful-looking. She was also very rich; her father manufactured auto parts. We—" Again I sighed. In spite of myself, I was speaking lower, slower, unable to sustain the impersonal glibness I'd first achieved. "We got married just about the time my so-called career in pro ball was winding up. I'd always intended to go into coaching. I'd assumed that when I'd finished playing, I could get a coaching job, maybe at some small college. And I probably could've done it. But instead—" I smiled wryly, lifting my shoulders. "Instead, I married a rich girl. I remember when we were still going together, we'd once joked about reading through the newspapers, looking for his and hers clippings—mine in the sports section, hers in the society section. She used to tease me, saying that her clippings were three times mine. I didn't realize until later that she'd actually measured them. Carefully." I took up my glass, draining it abruptly.

"So you lived in Detroit, you and your wife."

"Worse than that. I went to work for her father. I started out as an assistant vice-president."

"In charge of what?"

"Public relations, naturally."

She nodded, smiling wearily, finishing her drink. "That's quite a transition, from public relations to police lieutenant."

I began searching my pockets for money. Plainly, she was anxious to return home. And, suddenly, I felt as if I'd been talking too much. "I was in the M.P.s during the war," I said abruptly. "Luckily, I served with a man named Kreiger, who just happens to be my superior officer now."

When she didn't reply, we sat silently together for a long, reflective moment, each of us looking straight ahead, impersonally. I realized that I wanted to tell her more about the last of my life in Detroit: the terrible sense of futility I'd felt, aimlessly shuffling papers in my newly decorated office, constantly checking the clock, often driving three miles for lunch rather than face the daily ritual of the executive dining room. After a few months on the job, though, the realities of profit and loss caught up with me, and I was given my actual assignment: entertaining important visitors. After business conferences I'd take them to their hotel to pick up their baggage, then to the airport. Always there was time for a drink—at every stop, before every lunch, before and after every dinner. And always there was the necessity to be pleasant, talk football, gracefully pick up the check.

After two years of it I'd gradually slipped into the role of procurer. The right telephone numbers, I discovered, were as necessary as a credit card, or a constant smile, or an acceptable golf game.

I began arriving late at the office, after all-night sessions with clients. My afternoons and evenings became soggy, slow-motion spirals of smiling urbanity—always over a drink.

After three years of it, at age thirty-two, I realized that alcohol had slowly become essential to my precarious passage through each day.

After four years Carolyn and I agreed on a divorce. I couldn't stay in Detroit; she couldn't leave. She'd found another man. I didn't care. So we—

"—really think I should be getting home," Ann was saying.

I smiled at her—easing myself gingerly back into the present.

"Yes. All right." I dropped a few bills on the bar, and walked behind her, out to the street.

"You said last night that you lived nearby," she said, striding purposefully through the rain, head slightly bent, hands deep in the pockets of her raincoat.

"Just about a block and a half from you." I debated taking her arm.

"Would you like to come to dinner sometime?" she asked. "I— I'd like to show my appreciation."

"I'd be very glad to. I hope Dan won't mind."

"I hope so, too."

We'd stopped at a corner, waiting for a cab and a sports car to pass. As we stepped off the curb, I took her arm. Subtly, I felt her respond.

17

I parked across the street from Canelli's cruiser, three doors down the block from the Draper house. Signaling Canelli to stay put, I got into his car, sitting in front. Switching off the radio, I told him about Dan Haywood's statement. In another unmarked car, a young patrolman in plain clothes was keeping a lonely vigil, ignoring us. Watching him, amused, I realized that he was relishing his undercover role, imagining himself an inspector.

"Is anyone covering the back?" I asked Canelli.

"No, sir. Since this morning, there's only been a man at the front." He hesitated, then said, "It was Lieutenant Friedman's order, I think."

"Mmm." I glanced at him. "How're you and Friedman getting along, anyhow?"

"I haven't seen him since this morning."

"Have you bought yourself a jogging outfit yet?"

He grinned. "I'm waiting for Lieutenant Friedman. When he buys one, I will, too."

I nodded, opening the door. "That's probably wise. Well, I suppose we'd better get to work."

The Draper house was brightly lit, but three rings of the doorbell didn't bring a response.

"Maybe I should go around to the back," Canelli said in a low voice.

"You'd have to go all the way around the block. All these houses are attached."

"Maybe someone will let me through their—"

Suddenly, the door opened. Draper was dressed in an orange and black peony-printed Japanese robe. His feet were bare. His jowls were dark with a two-day beard. His long, thick hair was uncombed, falling tangled over one eye. He weaved unsteadily, squinting at us. Obviously, he was very drunk.

"Well, well." He stepped back, gesturing us inside with a deep, elaborate sweep of his arm. "The lieutenant calls. Come in, Lieutenant. Pray do please come in."

"Thank you." I walked directly into the living room, leaving Canelli to come up in the rear, bringing Draper along. Sitting down, I checked the time: it was 11:15 P.M.

"What is it, Lieutenant?" Draper asked, slumping into a deep armchair. "What brings you out in the rain, the night before the funeral of my late wife? Have you—" He burped. "Have you caught him yet?"

I slowly shook my head. "Not yet, Mr. Draper. But we're working on it. The reason we're here, in fact, is that we've uncovered some new evidence, and I wanted to—"

"It's been two days, you know." He burped again, then repeated ponderously, "Two whole days. My late wife would never understand such in—inef—" He cleared his throat. "Inefficiency. My late wife, you know, was a very efficient woman. Did you know that?"

"I can't say that I did," I answered briefly, settling back more comfortably. If he was stumbling into a talking jag, I couldn't do better than simply to listen, prodding him gently.

"Oh, yes—" He nodded, eyes owlish, lips loose. "Yes, Susan was very eff—efficient. And filled with convictions, too—absolutely stuffed, if that's the word I want. Loaded, maybe—absolutely loaded. She was a member of"—he held up five widespread, unsteady fingers—"of the League of Women Voters—" The index finger folded. "And the University Women. That's two. In fact, she was al-most president of the University Women, except that our house em-barrassed her. And, of course, me. I embarrassed her, badly. Very, very badly." He examined his fingers, frowned, and finally folded a second finger. "The Sierra Club, too. She was an incredible conser-vationist—absolutely incredible. Even before conservation was the thing to do." The hand dropped heavily into his lap, forgotten. "She was also an organic gardener," he said solemnly. "Did you know that?"

"I—"

"She grew tomatoes the size of cantaloupe, and cantaloupe the size of—of—" He hesitated, frowning.

"Of basketballs?" Canelli supplied helpfully.

As Draper twisted jerkily, facing his new inquisitor, I frowned at Canelli, shaking my head. When Draper finally turned back to me, Canelli shrugged, lifting his eyebrows to me, apologizing si-lently.

"Basketballs," Draper pronounced, "aren't edible. Even my wife—my late wife—can't grow a—*couldn't* grow an ed—edi—edi-ble basketball. Even with her frigging compost pile. Did I ever tell you about her compost pile, Lieutenant?"

"No, you didn't."

"Did I ever show it to you?"

"No."

"Hmm." As he stared at me, he was frowning deeply, deciding something. "I should show you her compost pile," he said finally. "A lot of people, you know, have never seen a compost pile." He burped. "Have you ever seen a compost pile?"

"No."

He turned to Canelli. "Have *you?*"

"Well, as a matter of fact, my aunt has one. She's an organic gardener, too, and—" Catching my expression, Canelli broke off abruptly.

"Susan's compost pile had a lot of significance for her," Draper said, his voice sloppily ironic. "A lot more significance than you might think, considering that it's just a lot of garbage and horseshit, all mixed together. In fact, I remember telling her once that she thought more of that pile of horseshit than she did of me." He looked up, assessing my reaction. "I was kidding, of course." He paused, sighing dolefully, dropping his eyes to look down at his feet. "I'm a little gassed," he said. "Tomorrow, you know, is the funeral. I'm not looking forward to it. I don't even have the right kind of a suit. I've only got one suit that matches, and that's brown. I mean, it's a light brown, not a dark brown. Everything else is sports coats and slacks. That's probably because I'm a free-lance photographer. As opposed, for instance, to a regular, working, respectable photographer."

"People will understand Mr. Draper," I said soothingly.

"Her parents are going to the funeral," he said, scowling now. "They arrived last night, and they're making all the funeral arrangements. They called tonight, in fact, to say that they'll be picking us up tomorrow at precisely ten A.M., in the undertaker's limousine. Actually, of course, they'd just as soon I didn't go. They'd *rather* I didn't go. They think that I—" He broke off, craftily clamping his jaw.

"They think that you what?" I asked quietly.

"They think that I was responsible."

"For her death, you mean."

He didn't answer.

"You *were* responsible. You said so yourself. Do you remember?"

He sank deeper in the chair, inert. With his head bent, his hands lying limp at his sides, I thought he'd passed out. But as I was arching my neck aside, trying to look into his averted face, he seemed to rouse himself.

"When I was eight years old," he mumbled, "I left the gate unlocked, and our dog got out. He got killed. When my mother heard him howl, and saw him dragging himself into the gutter to die, she screamed at me that it was my fault. She loved that dog. Every day she used to brush him. Every single day. I remember that I used to feel jealous sometimes, watching her cooing, brushing that dog. Once, when I was mad at my mother, I remember saying that I wished the dog would die. She was brushing him when I said it. She whirled around, and for a second I thought she was going to hit me across the face with the brush. Her eyes, I remember, were wild. And her hair stood out from her head, like a witch's. And those dog brushes, you know, have wires sticking out, like porcupine quills." He lapsed into silence. Then: "It's funny, but today I've been thinking about that dog, dragging himself into the gutter. His back was broken, so he could only use his front legs. And all the time he was howling. At first it was a very loud howling, so that everyone in the block came out to look. By the time he'd reached the gutter, though, it was just a low crying. And then he died."

"Did your wife cry out when she died?" I asked, pitching my voice very low.

"I don't know. I don't think so. I didn't hear her." His voice was remote, as if he spoke from the depths of a trance. He sat motionless, chin sunk on his chest.

"We have a witness," I said. "He saw your wife leave the garage and turn into the tunnel entrance. He didn't hear her cry out. He must've been there, across the street, during the time she was murdered. But he didn't hear a thing." I paused, then added, "He didn't see anything either, Mr. Draper. He was parked for some time, but he didn't see anyone except your wife, either entering or leaving the entrance of your house."

Watching him, I realized that the significance of what I'd said wasn't registering. And now his head twitched, still with his chin propped on his chest. He seemed to be dropping off to sleep. I exchanged a glance with Canelli. I nodded to him, hopeful that a new voice would rouse the suspect.

"What the lieutenant is saying," Canelli said loudly, "is that it looks like whoever did the job was hiding in the shrubbery, waiting for your wife. Like, he must've known she'd have to get into the house through the front door, instead of the garage. See?"

I realized that Draper was chuckling softly to himself. "I heard a joke once," he said, "about cantaloupes the size of basketballs. Or maybe it was watermelons. Anyhow, it was about this girl who—"

"What did you do when you first heard your wife downstairs in the garage?" I interrupted. "Did you get out of bed?"

With great difficulty he roused himself, tossing back his theatrically long hair, painstakingly squinting at me. "Did you say you wanted to see the compost pile?" he asked. "I can't remember."

I sighed. "Mr. Draper, I want you to concentrate on what I'm going to say. Now—" I paused, hopeful that my silence would focus his attention, yet doubtful that I would succeed. "Now, we have new evidence—a statement by a witness—that contradicts some of the things you've been saying concerning your movements on the night your wife was murdered. For instance, you say that you left the house through the garage, then found your wife's body, at about one-thirty A.M. Now, this new witness's testimony, if it's true, refutes that. Do you see what I'm getting at?"

He began to nod, then reversed himself, loosely shaking his head. His eyes were heavy; his head was sagging. His expression was utterly blank. He hadn't understood a word I'd said.

I got to my feet, indicating with a slight movement of my head that Canelli should remain seated. "Do you mind if I have a look around your house, Mr. Draper?"

His gaze suddenly sharpened, craftily suspicious. "Why? What for?"

"I want to retrace your movements on the night of the murder. I'd also like to take some of your clothing with me, for laboratory analysis."

"You think I killed her." His voice was expressionless, his eyes round and empty. His mouth was pursed in a childlike pout.

"We don't know who killed her, Mr. Draper. We do know that it's necessary to cross check your movements on the night of the murder. You—"

"You'll find blood, you know. I found blood myself, on my shoes. My pants, too. I must've been down on my knees. After that, I don't remember anything, until I was phoning. I don't know how I got back in the house."

"So you've said." I gestured toward the hallway. "Can I look around?"

"No."

Regretfully, I drew a deep breath, watching him gather himself for a bout of alcoholic belligerency.

Should I give him his rights? Ask him to get dressed? Should I take him downtown? Now was the time to decide. I couldn't search the premises without his permission. I could only take him away.

And the little girl. We'd take her, too. Instead of attending the funeral tomorrow, she'd be in the Youth Guidance Center, along with the delinquents, the subteen heroin addicts, the suddenly orphaned, the unclaimed and the unwanted.

But she'd at least be spared her mother's funeral.

Now Draper was glowering up at me, his face flushed, his eyes hot. Seeking a means of keeping him off balance, I decided to ask, "Do you have a leopard's head downstairs in your garage?"

Puzzled, he said, "Yeah. Why?"

"Can it be seen from the sidewalk?"

He smiled craftily. "If the garage door's open, it can. I bought that head for twenty-five dollars, at an auction. I was going to use it for a prop. I *did* use it, in fact."

I turned abruptly to Canelli, gesturing him to his feet. Pivoting back to Draper, I said, "We'll let you go to bed now, Mr. Draper. You're leaving for the funeral at ten tomorrow morning. Is that it?"

He nodded sadly, his sudden flare of bloodless belligerency past. "That's it, Lieutenant. I'm afraid that's it."

18

"Now what?" Canelli asked, walking beside me as I made for my car.

"Now we put someone at his back door, then see what happens. He knows we suspect him. Let's see which way he jumps." I pointed to his cruiser. "You make the call, then we can talk."

I watched Canelli put in the call, then speak briefly with the patrolman on stake-out. I kept my eyes on Draper's house, watching his shadow leap restlessly across ceilings. Once he stooped at the front windows, peering out unsteadily.

I'd often tried to imagine what a suspect was thinking, feeling, fearing. Watching Draper now, I was trying to conjure up what terrible phantasms must be tearing at his consciousness. It had been almost forty-eight hours since she'd died. For two days he hadn't been out of the house. For two days he'd been casually encountering her effects, caring for their daughter, perhaps sponging the blood from his clothing, rechecking the hiding place he'd chosen for the weapon and the missing billfold.

If he'd killed her.

Did he still have the weapon and the billfold? Without them, tied to him, we'd never make a case. The bloody clothing he'd already discounted. The bloody smear on the doorframe wasn't proof of anything. He'd been smart enough, or lucky enough, to tell a consistent story that covered his own inconsistent first statements.

Had he killed her?

Was Dan Haywood telling the truth?

Even dead drunk, Draper hadn't really stumbled. He hadn't damaged his position, and might have actually strengthened it. He'd accepted our suspicions without surprise or distress. He'd—

My car door opened. Canelli flopped into the seat, noisily exhaling.

"All set?" I asked.

"Yessir. Randall's already rolling. Should be here in ten minutes. Is Draper still in there?"

"Yes. He's wandering around."

"Do you really think he killed her?"

"If the Haywood boy's telling the truth, it has to be Draper."

"If."

"Don't you believe the boy's story?"

"Jeez, I don't know, Lieutenant. It's your baby, not mine. I never even laid eyes on the kid. The only thing is, it seems like nothing Draper's said has really been contradicted by evidence. On the other hand, that thumbprint blew the kid right out of the water."

"It blew his first story out of the water."

"They change their story once, though, there's no reason they can't change it again. I mean, I always figure that— *Say.*" He snapped his fingers, interrupting himself. "Say, I almost forgot what I was going to tell you, about the Manley thing."

"What's that?"

"Well, me and the lieutenant leaned on that Swanson chick, like you told me. And—"

"How'd it go, by the way?"

He thought about it, frowning. Finally he said, "I guess I'd have to say that it didn't go too good. I mean, we couldn't shake her. She wouldn't even admit that Valenti was the kid's father, which would've gone a long way toward establishing a motive."

"She had other motives, though. Jealousy, for one. What about that phone call? Did she admit calling?"

"She won't budge on that, either. She's tough. Real tough. The only thing I can say, though, is that I could see her doing the job."

"By herself?"

"She could've just walked in with a gun, and started playing it by ear. She could've got the Manley girl to tie Valenti to the bedpost. Then maybe she shot the girl, then tortured Valenti, and finally killed him."

"But you couldn't shake her story."

"That's right," he admitted. "I mean, I'm just talking about how it *could've* gone, not the way I think it went, especially. But anyhow, what I wanted to tell you about was when I took Swanson home. At first I was just going to dump her out in front of her building. Then I figured what the hell, I may as well take her inside, which I did. So then, instead of going right back to the car, I figured I'd go around the corner and buy myself some sunflower seeds. See, I been trying to quit smoking, so I been eating sunflower seeds. I bet I eat three of those fifteen-cent packs a day, which turns out to be as much money as cigarettes. But—"

"What's the point, Canelli?" I glanced at my watch, yawning. The time was almost midnight.

"Well, the point is that when I was walking back to my cruiser, I happened to notice a white VW bug parked around the corner from Swanson's apartment building. So I thought what the hell, I'd copy down the license number and run it through MVB. And guess what?"

"I give up, Canelli. What?"

"Well, the car belongs to Dwight Kellaway, who I remembered reading about in your interrogation report." He hesitated, looking at me tentatively. Then: "Do you think it's anything?"

Imagining meek, mild-mannered Dwight Kellaway committing murder for the love of brash, brassy Jane Swanson made me grin. Whereupon Canelli's expression of hopeful anticipation began to fade. I said, "It's probably a coincidence that Kellaway owns a white Volkswagen, but you might as well check it out. It's a point of inter-section, as they say in the criminology textbooks. Why don't you see if you can get hold of the car, first thing in the morning? Maybe you can pick it up before the nine A.M. briefing. Then run it through the lab. You can tell Kellaway that you're acting for me, eliminating him as a suspect. He's a good-natured guy; you shouldn't have any trouble with him."

"Okay. Will do." He gestured toward the Draper house. "What about this, in the meantime?"

"I think that I'm going to try to get a search warrant tomorrow morning, then make it a point to be here at ten. I'd like to see Draper's reaction, knowing that he'll be at the funeral while I'll be searching his house."

"Hey, that's pretty smart, Lieutenant. Psychological warfare. If he's got anything to hide in there, he's going to be sweating bullets."

"Let's hope. After I finish here tomorrow, I'll check with you on Kellaway's white Volkswagen. Maybe he murdered Valenti to protect Jane Swanson's virtue. Stranger things have happened."

"I suppose so." He reached for the door handle. "Do you want me to stay here and get Randall settled?"

"It'd be a good idea. At this time of night you're going to have trouble getting a stake-out set up, with all those backyards adjoining. You'd better see if you can find someone still awake, and go through their garage."

"The trouble I always have," Canelli said ruefully, "is dogs. It's dogs at night, and kids during the daytime. Well—" He sighed. "Goodnight, Lieutenant. Maybe by this time tomorrow we'll have both cases in the bag. I hope so. I haven't done my Christmas shopping yet."

I smiled, starting the engine. "Goodnight, Canelli. I'll see you tomorrow. Thanks."

19

Kreiger used a thick forefinger to flick back his cuff, glancing at his watch. The time, I knew, was precisely nine A.M.

"Is Canelli coming?" Kreiger asked, his impersonal look circling the small group of inspectors.

"Maybe not," I answered, explaining that Canelli had gone directly from his home to pick up Kellaway's white Volkswagen. I next took a few minutes to summarize the Manley case, careful to address Culligan, who was still in charge of our investigation at the scene of the crime. During the entire time I spoke, Friedman had been grunting noisily, shifting his bulk heavily from side to side, rooting first for a cigar, then for a match. Now he was lighting his cigar, never once having glanced at me. But as I finished, he was the first to speak.

"Personally," he said, pausing to puff, frowning at the cigar, then puffing again, "personally, I'm convinced that this Kellaway just isn't the homicidal type. Not only that, but I feel that you're all overlooking my candidate, Al Goodfellow. I admit I've never been at the scene of the crime, and tracked through all that talcum powder, et cetera, but it seems clear to me that, first, there were probably two or more murderers involved and, second, that the motive for the crime wasn't your standard breaking and entering, or a crime of passion, or whatever. Valenti was tied up like a steer on a meat hook. That took some muscle. And he was tortured. That took personnel."

"Unless," I said, "the murderer—singular—broke in, took them by surprise, and forced the girl to tie Valenti to the bedpost. Then the murderer could've made the girl watch while he tortured Valenti. If he was looking for money, that's probably what he would've done. And then maybe the girl came for him, and he shot her, then shot Valenti."

"The girl was shot in the back, though," Culligan put in sourly.

I'd forgotten that, I admitted.

"Well," said Kreiger, turning to Friedman, "what *about* Goodfellow? What's he say?"

"Frank and I decided we'd rather talk to you before we brought him in. I mean, it's always such a hassle, with those lawyers of his. Plus the D.A. always groans very loudly, as we all know. However, yesterday, I talked to two or three of Goodfellow's customers, and one of his subordinates. And they all agree that Valenti was very definitely on Goodfellow's shit list. So it would've been just a matter of time, they all agree, before Goodfellow sent a couple of his boys around to talk a little sense to Valenti."

Kreiger considered, finally saying, "I'll talk to the D.A. sometime before lunch. Meanwhile, if you can spare the time, keep digging on Goodfellow. We might be able to—"

His buzzer sounded. Twirling in his chair, he picked up the phone. He listened for less than half a minute, periodically grunting. After a perfunctory "Thanks" he hung up. Swinging back to us, Kreiger said, "That was the lab. Except for a lot of marijuana crumbs, they couldn't find anything incriminating in Bruce Manley's car. They don't have anything on the Haywood car yet, plus or minus. Nothing on Walter Manley's cars, either."

"Where's Bruce Manley's car now?" I asked.

"Haskell returned it about midnight," Friedman said smugly. "No sweat. As I predicted."

"The lab also said that Canelli called in. He's bringing Kellaway's car downtown."

"I wonder if he had any trouble," I said.

"Probably not," Friedman offered. "If I were a murderer, I don't think Canelli would worry me much. In fact, I think I'd be reassured, dealing with Canelli."

Kreiger surveyed Friedman with a chilly look to which Friedman seemed entirely oblivious. For a long moment no one spoke. Finally the captain said shortly, "Is there anything else on the Manley-Valenti thing?" He turned to Culligan. "What about physical evidence—prints, for instance?"

Culligan scowled, shifting irritably in his chair. "We haven't been able to get beyond the two victims, Bruce Manley, Billy Mitchell and the cleaning woman. We have at least five sets of unclassified prints, but we can't put a name on them. Or Sacramento can't, anyhow. By tomorrow, or maybe this afternoon, we should hear from Washington."

"What'd the cleaning lady have to say?" I asked.

"Absolutely nothing."

"I'm beginning to wonder whether it's going to turn out to be one of those irrational things," Friedman said. "A couple of hopped-up hippies could've just wandered in off the street and done the job for kicks. Maybe they were looking for drugs, and Valenti pulled a gun, which the hippies took away. Then they could've got inspired, and decided to try a little torture, just for laughs. When you really think about it, this case has everything except 'Pigs' scrawled in the victims' blood on the outhouse door."

"You could be closer than you think, Pete," the captain said thoughtfully. "After all, Valenti was dealing. Given that, anything could happen."

"What about the white VW?" I asked. "It was parked, apparently. Waiting. That sounds like premeditation."

Everyone seemed to shrug in indifferent unison.

"What do you think of Walter Manley as a suspect, Frank?" Kreiger asked.

"He was being blackmailed, so he had a motive. He had the opportunity, too—and no alibi. Theoretically, he could've done it. Actually, I'm inclined to doubt it."

"He certainly wouldn't kill his own daughter," Kreiger said thoughtfully. "Not intentionally, anyhow."

"Well, it's happened before. Or, possibly, Valenti could've killed the girl. Then Manley could've killed him. After all, we don't have much real proof of any actual sequence of events. We don't have a make on the bullets, either, and we don't have the weapon. It's all theory." I glanced at my watch: 9:25. "I'm going to leave in fifteen minutes. If I can get a warrant, I want to search the Draper house. And I want to be there before he leaves, to see how he reacts."

Glancing at his watch, Friedman grunted skeptically. "You're dreaming. In my whole career in law enforcement, I've never gotten a routine search warrant before ten-thirty."

"I still want to be at Draper's by ten. Haskell's at the judge's chambers, waiting for the warrant. He's going to bring it to the scene."

"Good luck. I'll bet—"

"I think we should be thinking a little more about Valenti's drug involvement," Kreiger interrupted impatiently, a note of finality in his voice. "God knows, we haven't got much else—just a few unsavory characters, a rich father and some kind of a starving writer who just happens to drive a white Volkswagen."

"When we do get on the right track, though," I said, "that talcum powder should help."

"In the meantime, there isn't much we can do except keep on like we're going." Kreiger turned to Markham. "What about the Draper thing, Jerry?"

As I turned to listen to Markham, I was aware of a slight, guilty sense of anticipation. I'd tried—really tried—to catch him before the briefing, forewarning him about both Arthur Haywood's lawyer and Dan's decisive change of story. But having been unable to catch him, I could now plainly recognize in myself a smug, sadistic pleasure, thinking of the surprise I had for Markham.

When Markham had finished his summary, concluding that Dan was our major suspect, everyone turned expectantly to me. I drew a deep breath, then dropped the bomb. I finished with the Draper interview, explaining directly to Markham that I'd tried to reach him last night. Which, of course, only made matters worse.

Although Markham was flushed, plainly angry, his eyes were steady, his voice dead calm, as he said, "Your case against Draper is only as good as that kid's word. Which I don't happen to think is very good."

"It explains the fingerprints, though."

"Maybe." There was a quiet, deliberate challenge in his tone.

I sighed, then said, "I might as well tell you the rest of it. Arthur Haywood, the boy's father, has hired a lawyer, who'll probably press charges of undue harassment against both you and me. Unless, of course, we can solve the case, and take the heat off everyone." I turned to Kreiger. "I didn't have a chance to tell you about the lawyer. But it could be coming. Unless, as I say, we get lucky."

"I thought you and I had agreed," Kreiger said slowly, "that you were going to concentrate on the Manley thing, and let Markham handle Draper." He was obviously displeased.

"I—"

"What I don't understand," Markham said, pretending puzzlement, "is why you stopped at the Haywoods' in the first place." He smiled, smoothly. "It sounds like you were mostly interested in talking to the mother. Which I can understand."

Pointedly ignoring him, feeling the quick rise of anger, I turned to Kreiger, again glancing at my watch. "Listen, I've got to go, if I'm going to catch Draper."

"Shall I go with you?" Markham asked, still smoothly.

"That's up to you," I said shortly, rising to my feet. I suddenly felt awkward—defensive, ill-at-ease, unsure.

"You'd better stay here," Kreiger said to Markham, "until we see which way Mr. Haywood's going to jump." And to me: "Come right back here, Frank, if there's nothing popping. We'd better get some of this thrashed out."

Mumbling something about a funeral being a good hunting ground, I left hurriedly.

20

I cruised slowly past Sigler, sitting alone in an unmarked car. I pulled to the curb in front of Cindy Wallace's house, parking directly across the street from the Draper residence. The time was exactly 9:55. Haskell had just contacted me to say that the judge was sick with a cold and fever. Wearily I'd instructed Haskell to try another judge, then leave the warrant on my desk, where I'd pick it up when I returned to the office. Friedman had been right; I should have known better than to drive halfway across the city without a warrant.

A cold gray rain was falling. I slid down inside my raincoat, covertly speaking into my walkie-talkie, checking with Sigler, verifying that the back of the Draper house was covered.

"Any developments?" I asked.

"Negative. He came out about an hour ago, to get the newspaper. And—" I could hear Sigler stifling a yawn. "And that's it."

"How'd he look?"

"I couldn't tell. He had on a bathrobe."

"What about the little girl?"

"I haven't— Oh, oh. Look up the street."

A black Cadillac limousine had sedately turned the corner and was pulling to a stop across the street. An elderly couple dressed in mourning sat alone in the rear of the car. The uniformed driver was getting out, making for the Draper house. As the chauffeur crossed the sidewalk toward the tunnel entrance, I saw Draper's front door open. A little girl came out. She was dressed in a white plastic raincoat and gleaming black boots. Her blond hair was in a ponytail, tied with a bright red ribbon. She was carrying her own small umbrella, and she came slowly down the stairs, staring at the long black car. Behind her came Howard Draper, dressed in a brown raincoat, bareheaded. He was descending the stairs uncertainly, like someone sick, just leaving the hospital.

I got out of my car. Standing with arms folded, I'd tipped my hat back so that Draper could recognize me clearly. If I couldn't search his house, I could at least give him something to think about during the funeral.

The little girl had already reached the limousine; the chauffeur was gravely opening the door for her. Inside, I could see Susan Draper's parents, leaning forward. The woman was reaching out for the girl, groping.

Draper, eyes on the ground, had almost reached the limousine. He hadn't seen me. I took a step away from my car, at the same time raising my hand to my hat, ostensibly to set it at a slightly different angle against the rain, actually to catch his eye. Now the Cadillac was between us; over the roof I could see only Draper's head and shoulders. He was ducking his head, about to—

Suddenly he saw me. Jerking himself erect, he stared at me across the rain-glazed roof of the car. I could see him stepping back from the opened door; I could plainly see the chauffeur's face, politely puzzled. Inside the car, the three people sat motionless, watching Draper. For a brief moment action was completely frozen.

I slowly inclined my head, politely nodding to the suspect, smiling. Woodenly, Draper returned my nod. Then, moving stiffly, he lowered his head and entered the car. The chauffeur closed the door, circled the gleaming limousine and got behind the wheel. Slowly they were driving away. Behind a rain-streaked window I could see Draper staring at me fixedly with the gaunt, hollow-eyed look of a road-gang prisoner, shackled and chained.

I climbed back inside my own car, out of the rain. Suddenly, with peevish clarity, I realized that I'd come on a fool's errand. I should have simply instructed Markham to get a search warrant. Then I should have returned to the Manley case.

Because of a small, saddened woman named Ann, a stranger, I'd made a serious mistake last night, compounding a subordinate's earlier error in judgment. Now, this morning, I was still making mistakes. I was playing hunches—a sucker's game, bucking the odds.

All I had, still, was Dan Haywood's story, already once changed. The entire case was coming down around me. I could easily predict the agenda for the conference I'd soon have with Kreiger. Markham, as my subordinate, had improperly interrogated a minor, illegally entering the Haywood premises for the purpose of harassing the boy. Then, worse, he'd botched the job, scaring Dan so badly that he dared not tell the truth. Finally, worst of all, I'd conducted my own improper interrogation, with results that couldn't be counted as evidence, once Dan Haywood's lawyer advised him to deny everything.

Yet I'd gotten testimony that could break the case.

Or break me.

I lifted the walkie-talkie, instructing the man covering Draper's back door to check in. He identified himself as Kent Williams, a steady, dependable man of my own age who raised chinchillas, had been building a fiberglass sailboat in his garage for six years and was already amiably talking about retirement.

"Anything doing back there?" I asked.

"Not much, Frank."

"How long've you been on?"

"Two hours. I relieved Randall at eight o'clock. Draper came out only once, at about eight-thirty."

"What'd he do?"

"Just walked around their garden. They've got a pretty good-looking garden back here. It looks better in the middle of winter than mine does in the middle of summer."

"How'd Draper look?"

"Terrible. He was dressed in some kind of a Japanese bathrobe, and even from thirty feet I could see that he must've felt rocky as hell."

"Hung over, you mean?"

"Maybe. He just looked—out of it. He had a heavy beard, and he seemed to be walking unsteadily. He wasn't staggering, though. He just seemed out of it."

"If he felt that way, I wonder what he was doing taking a stroll in the garden at eight-thirty in the morning?"

"I wondered that myself. He didn't seem to be enjoying himself."

"Where are you, exactly?"

"I'm in the yard right next to Draper's, on the south side. We've got it all fixed with the owners of the house. You can come right through the garage; it's unlocked. You'll see a lath house; that's where I am. It's a good setup."

"I'll be with you in a minute."

I told Sigler to stay put. Locking my car, I went through the next-door neighbor's garage and out into their backyard. I paused for a moment just beyond the house, surveying the scene. Having been built originally as a tract, all the backyards adjoined, separated by fences that averaged five or six feet. Without exception, each yard was twenty-five feet wide, most of them about fifty feet deep. In the Drapers' yard were two sizable pine trees, several dramatically flowering bushes and large banks of lush ivy planted as ground cover. A flagstone walkway led from the house to a rear garden plot, doubtless the area where Susan Draper had grown her organic vegetables.

I walked to the lath house, fully aware that I could be clearly seen by dozens of residents peering down from windows fifteen feet above the ground. In a dark business suit, raincoat and hat, I felt uncomfortably conspicuous prowling the soggy neighborhood.

Slipping into the lath house, shaking hands with Williams, I looked out through the redwood slats.

"This is fine," I said. "Perfect."

"Except that I couldn't see more than his head and shoulders, because of the fence. I tried to stand on a box, but it didn't help much."

"What'd he do, exactly?"

Williams shrugged. "He just walked to the back where that vegetable garden's planted. He stood there for a minute. Then he turned and went into the house. Period."

"Was it raining?"

"Just sprinkling."

I surveyed the redwood fence, at least five feet high. Technically, I had no more right in Draper's yard than I had in his house, uninvited. Still, trespassing was a lesser charge than breaking and entering.

"I'm going to have a look. You stay here." I picked up Williams' walkie-talkie, checking with Sigler. Responding, Sigler's voice was garbled. Frowning, I turned up the volume, rotating the radio.

"That stupid thing takes spells," Williams said. "I could hear you fine, but I can't hear Sigler worth a damn. It just came out of the shop, too."

I asked Sigler to repeat, finally deciding that he was saying everything was normal at his post.

I unlatched the door and walked to the fence, unbuttoning my raincoat, deliberately keeping my eyes straight ahead, avoiding the stares of curious householders. A child's tricycle gave me a precarious foot up, and I awkwardly vaulted the fence, landing in an ivy bed. My feet sank deep into mud; the wet ivy clung unpleasantly to my ankles. Swearing, I stepped out of the ivy onto the flagstone walkway. Over the top of the opposite fence a German shepherd's head suddenly appeared. The dog's snarl was low, incredibly menacing. His yellow eyes looked more like a tiger's than a dog's. I unbuttoned my jacket, loosening my gun in its spring holster. I stood perfectly still, staring at the shepherd. To get his head above the fence, he must be standing on something. Therefore, he could probably clear the fence in a single leap.

If he came for me, my chances of shooting him were small. And if I shot him, the investigation would fuel a fire already too hot. Williams, fifteen feet to the rear, behind a fence, couldn't help.

For a full minute I stood motionless. The sound of the dog's snarling was lower, rumbling malevolently in his throat. His yellow eyes didn't waver.

Then, deliberately, I half-turned away from him, walking with slow, stiff-kneed steps toward the small vegetable garden. It was a tactic that had often worked for me: facing big, sure trouble, the best solution is sometimes to simply walk away, very slowly, without looking back.

As I walked, I listened for the sound of the dog's rush. If he came for me, I'd turn to face him, using my revolver as a club, shouting for Williams, certainly already poised.

But the rush didn't come.

I was standing beside the vegetable garden, staring sightlessly down at the shrunken brown stalks. Out of the corner of my eye I saw the shepherd. His stance seemed less taut. I turned my back on him, unconcerned now. Williams could guard my rear.

As I squatted beside the garden, I suddenly realized that my shoes were caked with mud. Hastily I straightened, craning my neck to see the back of my raincoat. It was a muddy mess from my shoes. The rain was coming harder now; water was dripping from the end of my nose. My feet were damp. I'd have to go home immediately, change my clothes.

I moved beneath the sparse shelter of a twenty-foot pine tree, using the palm of my hand to wipe my face. The dog, I saw, had gone, probably to his own dry doghouse.

Very slowly I scanned the thickly planted backyard. If the weapon was a steel pipe, it could be hidden anywhere. He could have walked to the rear of the yard simply as a blind. He—

I was staring at an eight-foot square of green tarpaulin drawn over a sizable mound and firmly staked down. The mound was close beside the rear fence, screened from the house by laurel.

He'd talked about the compost pile. Drunkenly repeating himself, he'd talked about his wife's pile of horeshit, blearily urging me to inspect it with him. Often, I knew, a criminal's offhand bravado actually masks an inexorable subconscious urge to confess.

I glanced around the backyard, checking Draper's rear windows. Nothing stirred. I stepped toward the tarpaulin, drawing back a corner. The compost pile was a sticky, oozing mass of dank brown slime. I loosened another corner. The pile was about five feet in diameter, probably three feet high. A half-hour's work with a slim metal probe would—

"*Frank.*" It was an urgent, hissing stage whisper from the lath house. Turning toward the sound, crouching, my eyes flicked first toward the Draper house.

Still dressed in his raincoat, Draper stood in a rear window. He held the drapes clutched crazily in each hand, pulled wide apart. Even at fifty feet, I could sense his surrender to madness. He was staring down at me like a wild-eyed Wagnerian fury. Then, abruptly, he released the drapes, blanking out the window. I stood for a moment, irresolutely. Draper was now dangerous. But I had no warrant, no legal means of getting to him if he refused me entrance. I couldn't—

The drapes flicked aside, revealing his head and shoulders. He was crouching down, probably kneeling on the floor. He—

Suddenly the large window shattered. A rifle barrel materialized among the sparkling shards. I dove for the pine tree, rolling up to my knees. A shot cracked; the tree trembled. He was using a big gun—a deer rifle. Another shot exploded in the mud just to my right. As I drew my gun, two quick revolver shots came from the lath house. A third rifle shot crashed into the tree less than a foot above my head. Quickly I risked a hand and an eye, snapping a shot at the shattered window.

"*Frank.*"

"Yeah. I'm all right. Sit tight. Tell Sigler the situation."

"I have."

"All right. Cool it."

"Right."

My pine tree was hardly a foot in diameter; protecting my head and vital organs, nothing more. I sat very still, my back to the tree, listening to the ragged thumping of my heart. I tried to gauge my chances of scaling the fence, ten feet away. With covering fire, I could do it. Without protection, my chances were small. Yet, now, I was hopelessly pinned down. At fifty feet, our pistols could hardly hit the window, much less the man.

I drew a deep, unsteady breath. "Kent?"

"What?"

"I'm stuck. Tell Sigler to send two men with rifles and tear-gas guns over in your yard, using the fence. They can cover me while I get out of here."

"Right."

"See anything moving?"

"No."

"All right." I stretched out full length on my stomach behind the tree trunk. Immediately I felt the wetness penetrate through my suit. Automatically glancing at my watch, I tried to estimate the time elapsed since Draper's first shot. Two minutes? Five? I couldn't be—

"Frank?"

"Yes."

"Here they come. They both have rifles. M-16s. Tear gas, too."

"All right. Tell them to start working on that window. *Both* windows. Keep firing until I'm clear."

"Roger."

I drew up my knees, crouching close behind the tree, holstering my pistol. I was thinking, a little wildly, that whoever had planted that pine tree, years before, had probably saved my life. Because Draper could shoot. He—

The high, savage crack of the M-16s shattered the silence. I hesitated only a fraction of a minute. Then, throwing myself forward, I was racing for the fence, still crouching. I gripped the flimsy redwood, throwing up a leg. Something splintered as I rolled over the top, flat and low, combat style. I fell heavily, my knee striking a trash can. Through the fury of the gunfire, I clearly heard my pants leg ripping. Rolling to my knees, I lurched back to the fence, crouching between two patrolmen. Both men wore flack vests.

"You got any more of those?" I asked, panting.

"No, sir. Sorry."

"They aren't much good against a rifle anyhow," Williams observed. "Not at this range. You all right, Frank?"

"A little scared, that's all." Automatically I was pinning my shield on my mud-stained lapel.

"He's a good shot," Williams said.

"I know."

"Hey," one of the patrolmen said quietly. "I thought I saw that curtain move."

"Has he shown since you started shooting?" I asked.

"No."

"Keep your eye on that back door. I don't want him getting out of the house."

"Yessir."

"I'm sorry, Lieutenant," Williams was saying. "It's that goddamn walkie-talkie. By the time I finally figured out what Sigler was saying, Draper was already at the window."

"I wonder what happened to the rest of them—the little girl?"

"What little girl?"

"Never mind. Christ, I've never felt so miserable in my—"

Markham and Canelli were coming along the fence, crouched low. Markham carried a shotgun; Canelli, a tear-gas gun. Both men wore heavy rubber raincoats, flack vests and riot helmets. Each man carried two gas mask containers, shoulder-slung.

"Jeez, Lieutenant," Canelli panted. "You look terrible."

Snorting, I drew my revolver. "I feel wet, if that's what you mean."

"Muddy, too, I'll bet."

Not replying, I turned to the two uniformed men. "Have we got a good walkie-talkie?"

"I have," said one of them.

I took the radio, talking to Friedman, who'd just arrived. After two minutes of cryptic haggling, we agreed that his men, using their cars as cover, would drop four canisters of tear gas into both the basement and the main floor, two canisters on each floor. If the suspect didn't come out, Markham and I would go inside.

As I was talking, Canelli had worked his way down the fence until he was crouched next to me. He looked faintly ridiculous in the flack jacket and helmet—like an overweight, dark-jowled Italian cupid caught in someone else's war, staring with round-eyed, disapproving innocence at the surrounding carnage.

When I'd finished talking to Friedman, Canelli touched my arm. As I turned to him, he said hesitantly, "I hate to bother you, Lieutenant, but I think you should know. You remember that white Volks—"

Two quick shots, then three more suddenly spat out a vicious, staccato quick-fire from the house next door. Splinters flew from the redwood fence; someone gasped close by, hit.

"He's at the kitchen window now," a voice was shouting.

"Nail him," I screamed. "Kill the bastard."

Three M-16s opened up, all on semi-automatic fire. Markham's shotgun thundered twice. The sharp, acrid smell of cordite was stifling in the wet, heavy air.

"All right," I shouted. "That's enough. Save it." I shoved the walkie-talkie at Markham. "Tell Friedman to get that tear gas in there." On my knees now, I turned toward Williams, lying on his back, staring straight up. Swearing softly, he was clutching at his left arm, just above the elbow. Between his fingers I saw a bright red stain spreading on his white raincoat.

"There's the gas," Canelli said. "Lots of it."

"Jesus," came another voice. "Williams got hit."

Other men, all uniformed, heavily armed, were lining the fence, crouching like soldiers along a hedgerow. I heard Markham calling for an ambulance. His voice was low, controlled. Williams was trying to sit up, still swearing. His lips were very vivid against his pale face. His eyes were large, his beard dark. I put my hand on his chest, with my other hand drawing Canelli close to me.

"Cut that sleeve away. Apply pressure. Keep him flat and warm."

And to Markham, I said, "What about the goddamn ambulance? Have we got one?"

"It's coming," he said shortly, his dark eyes steady, flat.

A rifle suddenly opened up—an M-16.

"What's that?" I called.

"Nothing," Markham said coolly. "An itchy finger." He handed me the walkie-talkie. Listening, I heard Friedman say, "Jesus, it sounds like a war back there. How bad is Williams?"

"Not bad, except for shock."

"You'd better be careful about bystanders."

Irritated, not answering that one, I asked, "How many canisters have you—"

A single shot sounded from the other side of the fence. A ragged spurt of M-16 fire answered, until I shouted it to silence.

"Anybody hit?" I called.

No answer.

Cautiously I raised my head above the fence. Tear gas eddied from the shattered windows. Inside that house, there was no way Draper could see—no way in the world.

"Here's the ambulance guys," Canelli said.

"Good. Give me your helmet and vest," I ordered. And to Markham: "Let's go in and get him."

Nodding calmly, his eyes still opaque, Markham slipped on his gas mask, testing it. He put the shotgun aside. As I was testing my own mask, clearing it, someone propped a trash can against the fence, steadying the can. Nodding my thanks, I looked at Markham, moving my head inquiringly toward the fence. He raised his thumb, indicating it was okay.

I paused a moment, drawing a deep breath. A gas mask, constricting both vision and breathing, always caused me a momentary spasm of claustrophobic panic. I was beginning to perspire. The world outside was tunneled into the plastic face plate of the mask. The sound of my own breathing rumbled through my head.

I stepped up on the trash can, cleared the fence cleanly. Dropping on all fours, I drew my revolver. Then I realized that I'd forgotten to reload. I'd fired twice. I had only four live rounds in my gun.

Markham dropped beside me, gathering himself. I was on my feet, head down, running—sprinting for the back door. Reaching it, I hopped on my left foot, crashing my right heel into the door, just below the knob. The door splintered. I was inside, stumbling, recovering myself. The CS gas was thick, stinging my neck and hands, damp with rain and salty sweat. Afterwards—immediately afterwards—I must go home, shower, change clothes.

We were standing close together on a narrow, cluttered landing. To our left was a short flight of stairs leading up to the kitchen. I put a forefinger to my face piece, gesturing for silence. We stood motionless. There was no scrape of furtive movement—no sound of coughing.

Two years before, a berserk veteran of World War II had barricaded himself in a downtown apartment, holed up with a gas mask, an M-1 and hundreds of rounds of ammunition. He'd waited coolly for someone to come and take him.

He hadn't coughed, either.

Slowly, placing my feet carefully, I moved up the stairs, hugging the wall. Behind me, Markham hugged the other side, so that I wouldn't crash into him, retreating. The thick, eddying gas clouds cast familiar household objects into eerie phantasms, fugitives from Inferno.

The kitchen door stood a foot ajar. I pushed against it with the muzzle of my revolver. An inch at a time, the door swung open, sucking slow swirls of the yellowish-white gas across the bright-patterned kitchen linoleum.

Draper sat flat on the floor, propped like a limp rag doll in an angle between a coppertone refrigerator and a gleaming white wall. His hands hung limp and lifeless between widespread legs. His eyes were open; his head was flung flat against one shoulder, as if his neck had been snapped. From his gaping mouth blood still oozed, staining his shirt front like a garish Christmas tie. A yard above his head, the immaculate white wall was splotched with irregular, surrealistic smears of bright red blood and pale, pinkish brain-bits. White fragments of skull bone dappled the still-dripping mess.

Beside him, on the glass-jeweled floor, lay the rifle. A bit of blood stained the muzzle. Beside the gun lay a single tooth, richly inlaid with gold, bloody at the roots. Recoiling, the rifle must have knocked out the tooth.

Swallowing hard, I motioned Markham to signal the others. For us, everything was now safe.

21

Friedman opened my car's right-hand door and slid in beside me, exhaling as he pushed back his hat. Across the street, press photographers were stoically hunched inside their raincoats, waiting for their first glimpse of Draper's blanket-covered body. The rain was only a light, dreary sprinkle now.

"You really do look like hell," Friedman was saying. "What'd you do, dig a foxhole?"

"I—"

"You should go home. Wash. Have a—" He caught himself. "Have a tall 7-Up. Let Culligan and Canelli handle that car thing."

"What car thing?"

"Didn't Canelli tell you? Between volleys?"

"Listen, Pete. I don't feel like—"

"All right, all right." He held up a placating palm. "The plain, unvarnished truth is that, in an incredible burst of speed, the lab found traces of Karen Manley's talcum powder in Kellaway's car. Traces of rug fiber, too. It has to be verified, but that's just a formality." He grimaced. "Canelli scores again. By accident, as usual."

"What's been done about it?"

"Nothing except a stake-out. Kellaway's still in his apartment; I just checked, in fact. But everyone was waiting for you to retire victorious from the field of battle. Which you have. With small thanks to the walkie-talkie chaps, apparently." He paused, eying me—waiting for me to speak. When I didn't respond, he said in a quieter voice, "I'd be glad to handle Kellaway personally. Except that it'll have to wait for a while." He gestured to Draper's window-shattered house.

I sighed, checking my watch as I reached for the ignition key. It was eleven o'clock. Incredibly, only an hour and a half had elapsed since I'd left Kreiger's meeting.

"Tell Canelli to meet me in front of Kellaway's apartment house at noon. Or, better yet, tell him to meet me on Stanyan Street, around the corner."

"You're an iron man, Lieutenant. A lesser mortal would be shell-shocked by now."

"I'm shell-shocked, all right," I said curtly, starting the engine. "I figure I'm out at least a hundred bucks in ruined clothing."

"You look it," he said dryly, heaving himself heavily out of the car. "You still haven't responded to my Hanukkah invitation, you know."

As I groaned, he again held up a hasty palm, backing away, mock-bowing.

"The funny thing is," Canelli said softly, "this guy sure doesn't act like a murderer." He was unbuttoning his jacket as we approached Kellaway's door. "He was very nice—very cooperative."

"If you can spot a murderer by the way he acts, you'd better patent the process." I motioned him to the opposite side of the door. After a quick glance up and down the hallway, I knocked firmly.

Immediately I heard the sound of footsteps. As the door opened I felt my muscles tighten. My jacket was unbuttoned, my service revolver loose in its holster.

Kellaway was dressed as he'd been the day before. He stood relaxed in the open doorway, his arms and legs slung at odd, loose angles.

"Hey," he said cheerfully. "The whole gang."

"Can we come in?" I asked quietly.

"Sure." He led us into the living room, gesturing me to the same psychedelic box I'd used the day before. Canelli, according to plan, remained standing.

"I hope you've got my car," Kellaway said. "I have to be at work in a couple of hours."

"What hours do you work, Mr. Kellaway?"

"Two o'clock to ten."

"Is that the shift you worked Monday?"

He opened his mouth to respond. Then, instead of speaking, he slowly moistened his lips. The light was dawning. His eyes narrowed. For a moment his jaw sagged, giving his face a fleeting look of vacuous stupidity. Then, again licking at his lips, he nodded slowly. His eyes were locked with mine.

"What time did you get home Monday night?"

"Ah—about ten-thirty, I guess."

"What'd you do then?"

"I started writing. I write every night, from about ten-thirty to about two-thirty in the morning. I thought I told you that."

"Were you here, in your room, all that time?"

"I—" He swallowed, his prominent Adam's apple bobbing noisily. "I went out about one, I guess it was. To the liquor store. I told you that, too."

"Did you walk to the store?"

"Certainly. It's just around the corner. Listen—" He shifted limb-by-limb on his makeshift couch. "Listen, what *is* all this, anyhow? I mean, I don't mind you taking my car to be checked. And I don't mind talking to you. But—" He flopped a long arm across his knees. "But I'd like to know, at least, what you've got in mind."

For a long, deliberate moment I studied him. His eyes were steady, his hands relaxed. Altogether, he was projecting a better than average image of puzzled innocence. I glanced thoughtfully at Canelli, debating. Finally I told Kellaway exactly what we'd found in his car—exactly what we suspected. Then I gave him his rights.

During the entire time I'd been talking, Kellaway's eyes hadn't once left my face. Now, as I finished, he gave a low whistle, moving his head in a slow, stunned arc.

"That is some scenario, Lieutenant. That is really some scenario. The way your script's going, I'll be doing page fifty in the pokey."

I spread my hands. "You can't account for your movements during the time of the murder. A white VW was observed at the scene. Your car contains unmistakable physical evidence placing you at the murder scene."

"Placing the *car* at the murder scene. Not me."

I surveyed him for another long, silent moment, again holding his eyes. And, again, his gaze didn't falter. Most detectives, whether they realize it or not, rely on the "eye test" above all else. I was no exception.

"Was your car parked on the street Monday night?" Canelli asked.

"Yes. Down about a half block."

"Was it locked?"

"Yes, certainly."

"According to the lab," Canelli said, "there weren't any marks of forcible entry on your car. No indication that the ignition was jumped, either. Plus, VWs have a theft-proof setup, just like American cars."

Helplessly, Kellaway shrugged. For the first time I saw a look of fear in his eyes.

"Does anyone else have a key to your car?" I asked.

He shook his head. Then, turning to face me squarely, he asked, "Why would I kill them? *Why?*" His voice slipped to a high, plaintive note, sounding almost like young Haywood.

"For money, maybe."

"Money." It was a tight, desperately derisive hoot. "You think I'd kill someone for *money,* for God's sake?" He shook his head like someone sinking into shock. Then, in a lower voice: "Christ, I'm a refugee from the privileged classes, Lieutenant. My father is a capitalist. I admit that it's distasteful for me to ask him for money, at age twenty-six. But I'd a lot rather ask him than go out and commit murder." Involuntarily he smiled, ruefully. "Well, maybe a *lot* rather is a little strong."

"Have you often asked your father for money in the past year?"

"No."

"Have you *ever* asked him during the past year?"

He hesitated, finally saying, "Well, I did need an extra hundred when I made the down payment on my car."

"Did your father give it to you?"

He shifted uncomfortably, for the first time dropping his eyes. "Actually," he admitted, "my, ah, mother got it for me."

"Do you use drugs?"

"No."

"Narcotics?"

"No." His reply was edged with plaintive indignation.

"How about grass?"

"Well—" He shrugged. "Once in a while, if someone offers, I—" He broke off, glancing at me with quick apprehension. He'd just realized that he was confessing to a felony. I looked away.

"Does anyone else use your car, Mr. Kellaway?" Canelli asked.

He sighed, shaking his head.

"No one?"

"No."

"Are you absolutely sure?" I pressed him. "I'd advise you to think about it. Very carefully."

"I'm sure. I don't like to loan—" He paused, his eyes sharpened. He'd remembered something—or concocted something, protecting himself.

"I've only had the car for about nine months," he said slowly, "and the only time anyone ever drove it but me was"—he swallowed, glancing at me with transparent apprehension—"was when Jane asked to borrow it, a month or two ago."

"Jane Swanson, you mean."

"Y—yes."

I nodded thoughtfully. "We'll go have a talk with Miss Swanson. Meanwhile, I don't want you to leave the premises. Do you understand?"

"But I—I've got to go to work."

"At what time?"

"I leave about one-thirty. And now I don't even have a car," he said plaintively.

"It's only twelve-thirty. We've got an hour. We'll get back to you in time. Maybe I can arrange a ride for you."

We left him seated on his rumpled couch, looking about him with soft, sad eyes.

22

"Well," she said, "guess who's back?" Her voice was heavily sarcastic. She stood with hip thrust out, one hand on the doorknob, the other propped against the frame.

"Can we come inside, Miss Swanson? We have some questions to ask you."

"Ask them here."

"We'd rather come inside." I let my voice go flat.

"Oh, fer—" She flopped her wide-braced arm flat against her hip. Turning away, sighing loudly, she walked heavily down the hallway. She was wearing open-toed pink plastic sandals, sequin-studded. The apartment, I noticed, was even more disheveled than it had been the day before.

"Okay," she said, throwing herself petulantly into the brown armchair. "What now?"

"Is Mr. Rawlings at home?"

"No."

"Where is he?"

"Out."

"Where?"

"Shopping, I guess." She shrugged. "At least, he *said* he was going shopping. For whatever that's worth."

"Where's the boy?"

"He's out, too. They're getting some Christmas presents."

"Your son seems to spend a lot of time with Rawlings."

She snorted. "Whenever Dave starts to go out, which is most of the time, Jerry always raises so much hell that Dave *has* to take him. It's boredom, believe me. Not hero-worship. An apartment's no place to raise a kid." She surveyed the clutter with a bored, brooding stare.

Nodding noncommittal agreement, I sat silently, watching her with cold speculation. Soon she began to fidget, moving restlessly in the chair. She couldn't meet my eye for more than a few seconds at a time.

Finally I said, "We've just been next door, Miss Swanson. Talking to Dwight Kellaway."

"Big deal."

"Do you know Mr. Kellaway?"

"Sure. We're neighbors. Remember?"

"Do you, ah, spend much time with Mr. Kellaway?"

"What's *that* supposed to mean?"

"It means that I'm trying to find out how much time you spend with each other—how well you know each other."

"Oh." Lazy-eyed, she nodded derisively.

I leaned toward her, dropping my voice. "How many times a week do you see Mr. Kellaway, Jane? For how long, each time?"

She began to bluster, but couldn't quite make it. Finally, eyes sullenly shifted aside, she mumbled, "I guess I see him a coupla times a week. For two, three hours."

"What'd you do, when you see each other?"

"What'd you mean by that, exactly?"

"I mean, do you drink coffee—go for walks—just talk? What?"

"Well, mostly, I just go over there. Sometimes we drink a little wine. We listen to music, too. And just—talk." Her eyes flicked quickly up to mine, trying to assess the effect of her words.

"You're good friends, then."

She shrugged indifferently. "Neighbors—friends. Who knows?"

"Do you ever borrow things from Kellaway?"

"What kind of things?" She smirked. "Sugar?"

"I was thinking about his car. Did you ever borrow his car? His Volkswagen?"

Her first reaction was a glance of quick puzzlement. "Why d'you want to know that?" Her voice was low, cautious.

"Just answer the question, Jane."

"How come it's 'Jane,' all of a sudden? It was 'Miss Swanson' a coupla seconds ago."

"Sorry. I forgot my manners. Same question, different name."

Her sullen, sidelong look was scornfully contemptuous. "Big deal."

"The car," I said quietly. "Yes or no."

She shifted irritably. Flapping a hand, she said, finally, "Sure, I borrowed his car once. What's the big deal? Is there a law against borrowing someone's car?"

"How long ago did you borrow it?"

"A month ago, maybe. I forget."

"Why'd you need the car? Can't you use Rawlings' car?"

The cautious puzzlement was back in her eyes, watchful now. "Sure I can. But it just so happened that Dave's car wasn't working."

"So you borrowed Kellaway's car."

"Yeah."

"What did you do with the car?"

"I drove it, what'd you think?"

"Where did you drive it?"

Again she shifted uncomfortably. I was getting closer. But closer to what?

"What did you do with the car?" I repeated. "I want an answer."

"Why? What's so—"

"I'm investigating a murder, Miss Swanson. Maybe you've forgotten that, but I haven't. And we've just come into possession of evidence that makes it necessary for us to find out who's been driving Mr. Kellaway's car."

As I said it, I could see her eyes widen. Her hand, resting on the arm of her chair, was bunching into a tight white-knuckled fist. She sat arched forward in her chair, staring at me intently.

"Are you telling me that Dwight's car was used by the murderer?" Her voice was suddenly a harsh, hushed whisper. She knew something—something that frightened her.

I considered a moment, watching her closely. Then, very quietly, I said, "That's what I'm telling you, Miss Swanson."

"It—it was Dwight?"

"It could have been. It had to've been someone with access to his car—someone with a key, or the chance to have a key made." I paused. Then, with solemn emphasis, I said, "According to Kellaway's statement, the car has only been out of his possession once—when he loaned it to you. So, according to our physical evidence, the person we want is either you or your friend Kellaway. Or both."

"Or neither one," she whispered. She was staring past me with unfocused, shock-glazed eyes. Then, speaking in a dull, disembodied voice, she said slowly, "Dave made me borrow Dwight's car. His was broken down, he said, somewhere out on the Bayshore. He needed a car so he could pick up a spare part, and fix the trouble. At least"—she swallowed—"at least, that's what he told me."

I exchanged a look with Canelli. His full mouth was drawn up into an exaggerated, chin-puckered expression of cherubic surprise. Eyebrows raised, he was slowly waggling his head, thinking it over.

"I thought it was funny," she was saying, her voice still hushed. "Dave said that it wouldn't do any good for him to ask—that Dwight would never loan the car to him. And Dave *had* to have it, he said. We had a hell of a fight about it. We—" Her voice trailed off.

"But you *did* get the car," I prompted.

"Yeah, sure." Suddenly she seemed listless, indifferent. She sighed once, deeply. Then she forced herself to relax, leaning back in the brown plastic chair. She shook her head incredulously—as if she'd just discovered that she'd been cheated in a con game and had decided to take it philosophically.

"How long did Rawlings have the car in his possession?" I asked.

"A coupla hours, I guess. Who keeps track?"

I glanced at my watch. "When do you expect Rawlings back?"

"Who knows? He—" She broke off, struck by a sudden, stunning thought. "Jesus, he's got Jerry with him. He's got my kid."

Watching her, I made my decision: she was telling the truth. Her innocence, even her outrage could be faked. But not her sudden fear for the boy.

"Does Rawlings have a gun?" I asked.

She nodded. Under her breath she was muttering a string of obscenities, doggedly damning Rawlings.

"Where does he keep the gun?"

"Under his shirts."

"Show us." I jerked my chin to Canelli. Then, to the girl, who now seemed stunned: "Hurry up. Show us the shirts."

When she still didn't move, I grasped her elbow, roughly pulling her to her feet. Canelli was beside her, urging her along, her feet stumbling in her sequin-studded sandals.

I traced a twenty-five-foot cord, finally finding the phone on the floor, covered over by discarded newspapers. I dialed Communications, asked for Friedman. Informed that he was still in the field, I ordered that he be contacted in his car and connected to Jane Swanson's phone.

The girl was coming out of the bedroom, her eyes empty, her hands hanging limp at her sides.

"The gun's gone," Canelli said.

"What kind of a car does Rawlings drive?" I asked the girl.

"It's a Pontiac. A red GTO, with a black vinyl roof."

"How old is it?"

"Two, three years. I forget."

"Do you know the license number?"

"N—no." She sank down slowly on the coffee table, sitting round-shouldered, slumped, staring dully at the floor.

"Is the car registered to Rawlings?"

"I guess so."

"Do you know whether—"

"Here's Lieutenant Friedman, sir," came the dispatcher's voice in my ear.

"Pete?"

"Yes."

"Where are you?"

"On my way back to the office from the Draper thing—at about Fulton and Twentieth Avenue. What's up?"

Concisely I outlined the situation, asking for a DMV computer check of Rawlings' license number.

"You want me to drive over there?" Friedman asked. "I've got Markham with me."

"All right. The suspect could show up any time. We've got two men on stake-out here—in two unmarked cars. You'd better alert them to the new situation. I don't have a walkie-talkie. Be sure and tell them about the kid."

Friedman said, "Okay."

"If we can locate the car, we'll know where we're going. He could be on his way to Reno, for all we know. Besides, you can always contact me on this phone. I'll leave it off the hook. Whistle if you want me."

"I never learned to whistle loud. Just a minute." Then: "It's okay. Markham can whistle. You sure you don't want some reinforcements?"

"I don't think so," I said. "Rawlings'll have to come in through a narrow hallway, which is where we'll probably take him. It's close quarters. Too many men, and we could trip over each other. Maybe you and Markham can come up behind him, out of sight."

"Roger. I'll get back to you in a few minutes. Do you still want to leave that phone line open?"

I hesitated, then said, "I'd better hang up."

"Roger. Out."

I remained standing, still holding the telephone, staring at Canelli, who was leaning against the opposite wall. He looked vaguely uncomfortable in his rumpled suit and improbably creased hat.

"How long have they been gone?" I asked the girl.

"About an hour, I guess. I dunno." She was gazing down at her twisting fingers, clasped together on her thigh.

"They could be coming back any time, then?"

She didn't answer.

"Will he come through the front door?" I asked.

Head hanging, she nodded nervelessly. I turned to Canelli. "There's a back stairway opening into the kitchen. Make sure it's locked, just in case."

"Right."

"You'd better get out of sight," I said to the girl. "If he sees your face, he'll know something's wrong."

Her shoulders jerked convulsively as she choked on a short, bitter laugh. Slowly she raised her head. Her throat was corded painfully, her lips drawn back from tightly clenched teeth. Her eyes were wet.

"That's probably because I'm worried, Lieutenant. That's why he'd know something's wrong. My kid might be dead, in a few minutes. The idea worries me."

Looking at her coldly, I was thinking that she was a little late worrying about her child—several years too late. But pitching my voice to a neutral tone, I said, "There's nothing to worry about, Miss Swanson. Not if everyone keeps his head. Including you."

Again she choked, half-sobbing. Her eyes were bright, tearglazed with a bitter, bogus mirth. "There's nothing for *you* to worry about, Lieutenant. Nothing gets to you. I've known men like you all my life: cool, good-looking bastards with no more feelings than you can squeeze out of a Pepsodent smile. You're all alike. You're all—"

In my hand, the telephone suddenly rang. Startled, I automatically reached for the receiver, then recovered myself at the last instant.

"You'd better take this, Miss Swanson. Just in case. And you'd better get hold of yourself."

On her feet, she was staring fixedly at the phone, now beginning its second ring.

"*Take* it. I want everything to appear normal." I stepped up to her, thrusting out the phone.

At the beginning of the fourth ring, she answered. Instantly her eyes bulged. She was nodding frantically to me.

"Where are you?" she was saying. "Oh. Yeah. Well, I—

What?" She paused. Then: "I was in the bathroom. What're you—What?" Another pause. Eyes still wide, she was mutely begging me for a cue. I stepped close to her, whispering into her free ear, "Tell him to come here. Home."

"—whatever you want," she was saying into the phone. "Get some round steak, or something. Anything." Her voice was breathless, strained, unconvincing. Holding the receiver, her hand was knuckle-white. "No, nothing's wrong. I *told* you, I was in the bathroom. Just get the steak. Then come on home." Commanding him, her voice was edged with its habitual note of peremptory contempt. "And hurry up." She listened a moment, swallowing rapidly, searching my eyes for reassurance. Then, woodenly, she replaced the receiver in its cradle.

"How'd he sound?" I asked, taking the phone from her.

"I—I don't know. I couldn't tell." She sank down on the sofa. "Edgy, I guess. Jumpy."

"You sounded pretty jumpy yourself," Canelli said, standing beside her now.

Her hostile eyes flicked toward him as she automatically muttered a dejected obscenity.

"Where is he, do you know?" I asked.

"I think he's at Petrini's Market. Buying something for dinner."

Turning my back on her, I dialed Communications. Immediately, I was connected to Friedman's car.

"I've got the license number for you," he said. "CVV 306. It's already on the air."

"Where are you?"

"Geary and Seventh Avenue."

"You're within about fifteen blocks of the suspect's possible position. Petrini's Market."

"What'll I do?"

"Proceed to Petrini's. Canelli and I will meet you there. What channel are you on?"

"Tach Twelve."

"Right. I'll be checking with you in two or three minutes. Have another unmarked car assigned to this address, will you?"

"Roger."

I hung up and turned to Jane Swanson. "We're going to try and find Rawlings. It shouldn't be too hard. If we miss him, there're men outside this building. They'll apprehend him on the street, before he comes inside."

"B—but what about Jerry?" She spoke as if her lips were numb.

"Don't worry." Eying Canelli, I jerked my chin toward the door.

"I want to come. I won't stay here. You—you can't make me stay here." Eyes wide, she was beginning to babble.

"I'll leave a man with you. He'll keep you advised."

As she protested, I gripped her arm, digging my fingers into the flesh, hard. "You stay here. Right in this apartment. If you put your head outside that door, I'll book you for interfering with an officer."

I shoved her deep into the sofa, and left the apartment without looking back. As Canelli closed the door behind us, I could hear her cursing.

23

In the street outside Jane Swanson's apartment building, Culligan and Sigler were pulling to a stop in front of a fire hydrant. Verifying that Friedman had assigned them to me, I quickly outlined the situation, instructing Culligan to remain in the Swanson apartment, with his walkie-talkie hooked into Tach Twelve through Sigler, outside in their cruiser.

As I finished, Canelli was urgently beckoning me from our car, ready to roll.

"What is it?" I asked, slamming the door as the car jerked forward.

Canelli pointed to the radio, tuned to Tach Twelve. "Lieutenant Friedman. They've spotted Rawlings' car in the Petrini Plaza parking lot. The man and the boy are inside the car."

I clicked the mike to "transmit."

"Pete?"

"Yeah?"

"What's happening?"

"They're just sitting there. Doing nothing. I guess they're talking. Maybe arguing. The suspect seems to be waving his hands a lot. The kid is quiet, as if he's being disciplined."

I instructed Canelli to proceed to Petrini's at moderate speed. Into the mike I said, "The suspect could be going into the market.

You'd better maintain your position." I paused, then added, "He might go inside to shop, and leave the kid inside the car. We'd be home free."

"Sorry," came the laconic reply, "but the suspect's just been inside. He's getting ready to leave the area, I think."

Muttering an obscenity, I said, "We're proceeding up Stanyan, near Parnassus. We'll be with you shortly. Out." Leaving the channel open, I leaned back in the seat, braced against the car's sway. I forced myself to relax, conscious that my muscles ached with the dull, leaden weight of exhaustion. One way or the other, I'd soon be committed to another confrontation, too soon.

"Maybe Markham and the lieutenant can take him in the parking lot," Canelli was saying. "Before he gets under way."

"We'll be there in five minutes," I said. "Let's see what happens. With the kid involved, I don't want to—"

Friedman's metallic voice interrupted: "He's starting the car, Frank. We're down to our last ten seconds."

It took me three of the ten seconds to decide. "Let him go. Let's follow him with a rolling tail. If he heads for home, we've got reinforcements."

"Roger. How far away are you?"

"Eight, nine blocks. We're still proceeding north on Stanyan." Motioning Canelli to go faster, I called into Communications, confirming that Culligan, inside the Swanson apartment, and the three cars outside the building were hooked into Tach Twelve. Then, in a sentence, I outlined the current situation.

As I finished, Friedman's voice cut in: "The suspect is proceeding west on Fulton, Frank, just entering the Cole Street intersection. He's coming in your direction."

"He might be heading for home. If so, we'll apprehend him after he leaves the car but before he enters the building. All units, please verify."

As the verifications came over the air, Friedman's voice, tighter, interrupted: "He's approaching the intersection of Stanyan and Fulton, Frank. But he isn't signaling for a left turn. It doesn't look like he's going home."

"Maybe he's going through the park. Anyhow, we're just a block from Fulton. We should sight him soon." And to Canelli: "Turn left on Fulton, slow and easy, so we'll be heading west, like Rawlings."

"Check." Canelli jerked the car abruptly into the left-turn lane. Fulton was a half block ahead, mildly congested. A few drops of rain were spattering against the windshield. Ahead, the traffic light turned red, against us.

"We're stopped at Fulton, waiting to turn west," I announced into the radio.

"Keep on your toes" came Friedman's voice. "He's just entering that intersection."

And fifty feet ahead I saw the red GTO. The boy's head was clearly visible in the passenger's front seat. He was staring straight ahead, apparently untroubled.

Then, as if it were passing before us from stage left to stage right, the GTO was gone, disappeared in the wings. The traffic light turned green; our lane of traffic was moving.

"You go ahead, Pete," I said. "Pass him. We'll take over."

"Roger."

And as we turned into Fulton behind Rawlings, Friedman passed us, accelerating to overtake the red Pontiac.

"Keep about a half block back," I told Canelli. "We don't want to spook him."

"It doesn't look to me like he's going home," Canelli said. "I'll bet that Swanson chick scared him off. She sounded about as convincing as—as—" He shook his head dolefully.

"You're a pessimist, Canelli. I'm surprised you chose police work for a career."

He glanced at me doubtfully, then turned back to the road. "Well, the honest-to-God truth, Lieutenant, is that I started out to be a fireman. But I—"

"Lieutenant, this is Sigler."

"What is it, Sigler?"

"I just heard from Culligan, up in Swanson's apartment. Apparently Swanson's raising hell. Claims we're endangering her son.

She's threatening to sue. Everything. Culligan thought you should know."

"Tell Culligan to tell her that she's got no one to blame but herself. Out."

The GTO was pulling to the right lane, signaling for a turn. Almost a block ahead, Friedman was already into the next intersection. If he turned right, Rawlings could elude Friedman.

"I knew it," Canelli said. "He's turning on Park Presidio, making for the Golden Gate Bridge."

Into the mike I gave the suspect's new direction, then momentarily switched to Communications, outlining the situation, requesting State Police assistance at the Golden Gate toll plaza. As I switched back to channel twelve, Canelli said, "If the State Police don't already have a car at the toll plaza, they'll never stop him. He'll be there in just a couple of minutes."

"It's like I said, Canelli: you're a pessimist."

A hundred yards ahead, Rawlings was turning, sharply accelerating as he moved into the faster flow of parkway traffic. Seven or eight more blocks, and he'd be on the bridge approach, traveling nonstop at fifty miles per hour in the sparse early afternoon traffic.

"Where are you, Pete?" I said into the mike, bracing against Canelli's jolting turn.

"We're proceeding north on Fifteenth Avenue" came the terse reply. "We should be about even with him, one block over. What now?"

"I've radioed for the State Police to intercept him at the toll plaza. We'll be right behind him. I hope."

"Right. I'll be on Park Presidio in a minute. Maybe we should try to stop him on the bridge approach."

"At the toll plaza, he can't go anywhere."

"It's your ball game. But there could be a jumbo traffic jam." He paused, then said, "We're approaching Park Presidio now, traveling on Balboa, preparing to— Hell, we've got a red light at the intersection, and a bottleneck."

Two cars ahead of us, the GTO was midway into the Balboa intersection.

"There he is," muttered Friedman. "Big as life."

To Canelli, I said, "Pass these two cars. Get right in behind him."

"Check." He swerved abruptly to the left, cutting off a horn-wailing gray station wagon. Canelli was muttering indignantly as he passed the first car ahead of us, then drew even with the second, a bright red Ford driven by a blowzy middle-aged blonde. Rolling down my window, I motioned for her to fall back. Frowning, lips pursed, she was shaking her head vehemently. Over my shoulder I saw Friedman coming up fast, but still a full block behind us. Looking through the GTO's rear window, I could clearly see both Rawlings and the boy.

"Cut her off," I said shortly, withdrawing my arm, unwilling to risk attracting Rawlings' notice.

Traveling at almost fifty-five, Canelli suddenly cut to the right. I saw the blonde's broad, flat face contorted with rage as she braked quickly, falling back. Ahead I could see Rawlings glancing repeatedly into his rear-view mirror. The Lake Street intersection, coming up, was the last one remaining before the parkway emptied into the nonstop bridge approach. The traffic light was green. Contacting Communications, I fumed through a thirty-second delay, waiting to be connected to the single highway patrol car, just arriving at the toll plaza, barely three miles away. Finally I heard a garbled voice:

"—is Patrolman Stark, standing by."

I identified myself, then said, "How many outbound lanes are open?"

"Three, sir."

"Don't you have anyone else there? Any other officers?"

"Negative. I've requested assistance from one unit standing by at the northern bridge approach. He's proceeding across the bridge now."

"Do you have a description of the vehicle we want?"

"Yessir." He repeated the description.

"Can you place your car so as to block the suspect's lane while he's paying the toll?"

"I can try, sir" came the doubtful rejoiner.

I saw Friedman drawing up beside us, gesturing with a single upraised finger, eyes straight ahead. He looked like a well-fed tourist out for a Sunday drive.

"Have you advised the toll collectors of the situation?" I asked Stark.

"No, sir. I just this minute arrived." His voice was softened by a slight Southern drawl.

"Well, advise them. Get out of your car and explain what's happening. You've got about a minute. Tell them to stall—drop his money, anything. Then, while he's distracted, try to get your car in position. If you can't do it—if you can't block him—we'll take over. We're right behind the suspect. We'll get out of our car while he's paying the toll, and we'll apprehend him. Clear?"

"Yessir."

"Be careful. He's got a gun, plus the boy. Just park your car and slip out on the opposite side. Take cover. Out."

Friedman and Markham were still beside us, ignoring the indignant bleating of an orange Porsche. I switched to channel twelve. "It won't be long now," I said. Friedman grunted in reply. Rounding the last long, sweeping curve, I could see the line of tollbooths. Rawlings was already slowing sedately, making for the center of the three outbound lanes. To our left, Friedman was falling behind, helpless, trapped in a slower lane.

"Crap," I heard him mutter.

"Get in behind me," I said.

A horn blared as Markham obeyed. I could see Rawlings shifting from side to side in his seat, searching his pockets for a quarter.

Four cars remained between Rawlings and the tollbooth. To the right, partially concealed behind a huge wrecker, I saw Stark's highway patrol car. I realized that he had a delicate timing problem. If he moved too soon, Rawlings could simply make a quick U-turn, hopping the center barrier, heading back to San Francisco, spooked. Moving too late, Stark couldn't get through the right-lane traffic soon enough to reach the center lane, and the suspect.

Two cars remained in front of Rawlings.

I unbuttoned my coat, drawing my revolver. "I'll take Rawlings' side," I told Canelli. "You get the kid. Yank him out of the car and get him down on the ground."

"Right." Canelli's gun, a big Magnum, was on the seat beside him.

"Here we go," I said into the mike. "If he makes a break, let's aim for the tires."

"Right. Good luck" came Friedman's low voice.

Only one car remained.

Stark was moving out from behind the wrecker. A camper truck and a blue Cadillac were blocking him. Rawlings, arm extended outside his car, had reached the toll-taker's booth.

I opened the door. "I'm getting out. You stay with the car for a second or two, until I reach him. Then you move."

"Yessir. Good luck."

With our car still in motion, I swung open the door and jumped out, crouching low, stumbling as I fell to one knee, quickly recovering. Stark's car, I saw, was hopelessly blocked, out of it. Rawlings was fully stopped; the toll taker had dropped his money. I was rounding the rear of the GTO, still crouching, my shoulder touching the car's gleaming red metal. On the driver's side now, still crouching low, gun ready, I—

The car lurched ahead, tires screaming. Faintly I heard a child's startled, high-pitched voice. Friedman was beside me. As I raised my revolver, aiming for the Pontiac's tires, Friedman's gun thundered in my ears. I fired once, twice. The car swerved. Behind me, I felt the concussion of another gun's muzzle blast. From across the bridge came a black and white State Police car. Suddenly the highway patrol car braked, turning sharply over the dividing strip, bouncing, blocking two of the three outbound lanes. One of Rawlings' rear tires was thumping, flat—the right rear. The GTO swung toward the right, making for the one free lane. The highway patrolman moved with him, cutting him off. The Pontiac jerked to a stop, pinned against a low metal wall, two hundred yards ahead of us. I jumped for our car, sliding in beside Canelli, reaching for the microphone. As we moved forward, Canelli pointed ahead.

"He's got the goddamn kid, Lieutenant. Look."

The passenger's door on the Pontiac's right side was swinging open. Rawlings was clambering out, his left arm crooked tight around the boy's neck, his right hand holding a pistol.

"Take it easy," I ordered Canelli. "Drive slow. It's a different ball game now. He's not going anywhere."

"Except maybe over the railing," Canelli was muttering.

Glancing behind, I saw Friedman following closely. On either side, automobiles were already tightly impacted, their horns blaring. Shock-whitened faces peered from rolled-down windows; a few aggressive rubberneckers were already out of their cars. To my right, I saw Stark leaving his patrol car, taking cover behind a succession of stalled vehicles as he moved cautiously toward the GTO. He carried a short-barreled shotgun.

"Turn across the road," I ordered Canelli, "so we can have some cover." On the radio, I heard Friedman telling Markham to do the same. I was semaphoring my arm, signaling all vehicles to stop.

A moment later, with our cars parked bumper-to-bumper, approximately fifty feet from Rawlings, we were blocking all three of the bridge's outbound lanes. Keeping low, I slid from the car, followed by Canelli, grunting laboriously. Friedman and Markham were already crouched down behind their car. I motioned for Markham to join Canelli while I slipped behind Friedman's car. Cautiously raising my head over the car's hood, I saw that Rawlings had climbed up to the bridge's pedestrian walkway. He stood flattened against the four-foot railing, legs braced wide, holding the boy as a shield. The boy's head reached only to Rawlings' chest. A sniper could easily shoot the suspect through the head.

But Rawlings held a .45 automatic pressed against the right side of the boy's neck.

On the radio, Friedman was calling for assistance. Finishing the call, he tossed the mike inside the car, then drew his revolver.

"This," he said, "is a mess. Look at that traffic. In five minutes it'll be backed up all the way to City Hall."

"Did you call for a sniper?"

"Yes. I told Culligan to bring the kid's mother along, too."

"Why'd you do that, for God's sake?"

"It adds pathos," he answered blandly. "We've got kind of a combination hostage and potential suicide situation here. Relatives and clergymen help, sometimes."

"Sometimes not, too. Swanson's not exactly the mother of the year."

"Sorry. I never talked to her. You want me to countermand the order?"

"Never mind." And to Canelli: "Bring me the bullhorn."

Waiting for the horn, I kept my eye on Rawlings. He was standing perfectly motionless. His heavy features were twisted into a grotesque mask of wild, blind hatred. The boy was limp with terror, his throat working convulsively, his fear-numbed body racked with sobs. His head was bobbing loosely as he hung suspended, like a limp, lifeless puppet, from Rawlings' muscular arm. Now Rawlings jabbed at the boy's head with the muzzle of his automatic. I could see the boy wincing.

Next to me, Friedman was haranguing the bridge director, demanding that a single inbound traffic lane be blocked, reserved for police vehicles outbound from the city. Countless automobiles, immobilized, blackened the entire bridge approach.

Panting, Canelli was handing me a bullhorn. Behind us, the first squad car was pulling up, traveling against the inbound traffic, forcing its way. As Friedman briefed the two patrolmen, I clicked on the bullhorn, turning to the motorists behind us.

"Everyone stay in your cars," I said, talking against the blaring echo of my own voice. "Repeat: remain in your cars. Switch off your engines. We have a man with a gun—a dangerous situation. But if you stay in your cars, you'll be safe." I paused, then added, "It'll probably take some time to return the situation to normal, so you'd better plan accordingly."

Two more patrol cars, a police station wagon and an ambulance arrived. In one of the cars was a sniper, carefully carrying a scope-sighted M-1. Friedman dispersed the newly arrived men and their vehicles, tightening the ring around Rawlings. I beckoned for the sniper to join us, behind Friedman's car.

Now, gripping the bullhorn, I turned to face Rawlings, ringed by a ragged semicircle of police vehicles, each one sheltering two or three crouching officers. In five full minutes the subject hadn't moved. I noticed that the boy's pants were stained. Paralyzed by fear, he'd urinated.

Still behind Friedman's car, carefully placing my midsection in line with the door's center posts, I slowly straightened to my full height, exposing my head and shoulders above the roof. Holstering my revolver and resting the bullhorn on the roof, pushing the "on" button, I said, "This is Lieutenant Hastings, Rawlings."

He was twisting toward the sound, now facing me fully. I could see his hand tightening on the big automatic.

"Place the gun on the pavement, Rawlings, and step away from it. Let the boy go. You won't be hurt." I turned to the half-circle of police cars, saying, "As long as the subject remains where he is, I don't want anyone to fire. I don't want him harmed."

Most of the officers had heard it all before, and realized that I was speaking for Rawlings' benefit. In a stand-off situation, they would never fire without specific orders, even if they were fired upon. Their job was to take cover, aiming their weapons at the subject "in a threatening manner," quietly awaiting orders. It was all in the manual: page—paragraph—line—

I clicked off the bullhorn. Without moving my head, addressing the sniper whose rifle rested across the hood of Friedman's car, I said, "Take aim at his head. Have you got your scope sighted in for this range?"

"Yessir. I've just done it."

"Are you familiar with your weapon?"

"Yessir."

I glanced down at his face, strange to me. He was barely twenty-five. But his hands were steady, his eyes calm and clear. With his cheek snug against the rifle's stock, he looked convincing—steady enough for the job.

"What's your name?"

"Harrington, sir."

"When's the last time you fired that rifle—that particular rifle?"

"Three weeks ago, sir. I—"

"He's all right, Frank," Friedman cut in. "He can hit a dime at a hundred yards. I've seen him do it."

"Have you ever fired at a man, Harrington?"

Without taking his eye from the scope, Harrington drew a deep slow breath. "No, sir. Not with a rifle."

"Well," I said, "I hope you don't have to start now. If you do, though, I want that bullet right between the suspect's eyes. Otherwise, we'll have a dead kid on our hands. Clear?"

I saw him blink, then slowly swallow, twice. He'd put his uniform cap on the hood beside the rifle. I could see perspiration beading his forehead. But his voice was steady as he said, "Clear, sir."

I stared at him for a last long, searching moment. Finally I made my decision: if I had to order Rawlings killed, Harrington was my man.

Clicking on the bullhorn, I turned back to Rawlings. "Rawlings," I said, pitching my voice to a slow, steady note. "Put the gun down. Walk away from it."

"Screw you, Lieutenant." His voice was low and harsh—ominously steady, purposeful. Yet Rawlings' cold menace promised hope for the boy. Hostages are usually killed by mistake—irrationally, hysterically.

"You can't get away, Rawlings, and you know it. You're just making it hard on yourself."

"I think I can. I think you're going to give me a car. Unless you want this kid's brains splattered all over the pavement."

I tried to make my voice almost casual as I said, "Don't be dumb, Rawlings. The way things are now, you've got a chance. Nobody really knows what happened Monday night. Maybe you had a reason for what you did. Maybe not. But if you harm that boy now—here—you're finished."

"I want a car. Yours."

"Forget it."

"This kid's time is running out, Hastings. Another minute, and he's dead. One more minute."

"And the second after that, you're dead. When you fire, so do we."

"You're bluffing, Lieutenant. That's murder, in front of a thousand witnesses."

"Not if you fire that gun, Rawlings."

"I want a car."

"And I want that gun. Think it over, Rawlings. Take your time." Without moving my head, I spoke to Harrington: "Get ready. If I say 'fire,' that's it. You'll just have the one word—the one command. And the responsibility is mine—entirely mine. Lieutenant Friedman is your witness. Clear?"

"Yessir."

"It could be any second now."

"Yessir."

And to Friedman, I said, "What'd you think, Pete?"

"Wait a minute." He'd been speaking on the radio in a low, terse voice. Now he broke off, saying to me, "I've just been talking to the state policeman who blocked Rawlings' car. He's closest to the scene, barely thirty feet away, across the circle. And he doesn't think Rawlings has his gun cocked. It's a Colt .45 automatic, you know, with an external hammer."

"Thinking isn't good enough. Can't he be sure?"

"I don't know. Maybe he doesn't want to take the responsibility, and I can't blame him. You want me to move around there and look for myself, then call you on the radio? If that gun isn't cocked, we've got a big fat half-second to play with."

I hesitated. I had to know about the gun. But I desperately needed Friedman with me, for my own protection, and Harrington's.

"Let Canelli go," I said finally.

"All right." He beckoned for Canelli, who was now standing casually erect behind his car, one hand in his pocket, loosely holding his Magnum.

"I'm getting impatient, Lieutenant," Rawlings called. "I'm going to start counting. To ten."

"You may as well make it a hundred, Rawlings. We aren't moving. And we aren't giving you a car."

"You don't think I'll shoot the kid, do you?"

"Frankly, no." I turned my head slightly, watching Canelli's bulk slipping awkwardly from car to car. He looked like a fat, over-grown kid playing cops-and-robbers.

"Frank," Friedman said sotto voce. "Look behind."

Slowly turning, I saw Culligan picking his way through the crowd of cars, holding tightly to Jane Swanson's arm. Again facing Rawlings, waiting for his reaction to his girl friend's presence, I spoke softly to Friedman: "Tell Culligan to get her over behind my car. He and Markham can hold on to her."

"Roger."

As Friedman was signaling to Culligan, I saw Rawlings' eyes widen. He'd seen her.

Suddenly, wildly, he was laughing. "What're you doing, Hastings? Making it a goddamn family party, or something? Is she sup-posed to be a witness to the execution, or what?"

"No, Rawlings, she's—"

"Let my kid go, you goddamn son of a bitch." Screaming, she was pulling against Culligan, lunging toward Rawlings like a wild animal maddened by the rasp of a rope, kicking, gouging, spitting.

"Grab her, Markham. Help Culligan. Get her down behind the—"

As Markham moved quickly toward her, Jane Swanson sud-denly whirled on Culligan. Her free hand, clawing, ripped at his face, his eyes. Her knee came flashing up between his legs. Grunt-ing, Culligan exhaled, doubling up, eyes closed. As Markham reached for her, she pulled free. She was between the two cars, out of reach. Eyes wide, body tense, she stood at bay, trapped in the same circle that ringed Rawlings and the boy. Markham, coldly furious, stood poised between the two cars, ready to go for her. Rawlings' au-tomatic was moving in our direction, away from the boy's head.

"Hold it, Markham," I said. "Don't do it."

Beside me, I heard Friedman swearing earnestly. "This," he said softly, "could be a horse on me."

"Maybe not. Maybe she'll do our job for us."

"If she does, it'll be the hard way. I'm sorry, Frank. This isn't going to look so good in reports—for either of us." He was standing beside me now, watching the woman intently as she advanced on Rawlings, a single slow step at a time, oblivious to us. She held her arms rigidly at her sides, fists clenched. Her breasts rapidly rose and fell; her nostrils flared. Her gaze impaled Rawlings with the blazing, heedless, single-minded fury of a character out of Greek tragedy. Her lips were moving. Her words were inaudible, but her mouth curved with vicious, obscene contempt. Her eyes never left Rawlings.

The automatic was now aimed at the woman, who was advancing steadily. Her voice rose: "Why don't you shoot me, you lily-livered bastard? Are you too chickenshit to pull the trigger? Is that it? Even with a gun, you aren't good for anything except scaring kids. Because you aren't scaring me, you—you big-talking, milk-sopping, no-balls son of a bitch. You never *did* scare me, even when you were beating on me. All you're good for is standing in front of the mirror, wishing you were—"

"I'll kill you," he shouted. "One more step. Just one step, and I'll—"

"One step? Then what'll happen, little man? What'll you do with that big, hard black gun?" Deliberately she stepped forward, stiff-kneed. But now she stopped, facing him across one full width of a traffic lane, standing just short of the last yellow line. Her voice was lower, somehow strangely ominous as she said, "Was that the step, Dave? Or did you really mean the next step? Or is it really the step after that? Which one, Dave, before you finally figure out that you haven't got the guts to pull the trigger?" She smirked, taunting him. "Do you know how much you love that gun, Dave? You call it a rod —your rod, you call it. And you play with it, just like little boys play with their—"

"Shut up, you bitch," he was screaming. "Shut your filthy, stinking, slut of a mouth. You—you—" Suddenly wordless, he seemed to be gasping for breath, mouth torn wide, eyes bulging. His forearm across the boy's chest had loosened. The boy was sagging, knees bent. Now his head lolled at Rawlings' waist. Our margin was improving with every inch the boy's head came down.

But now, for the first time, the automatic was in plain view. The hammer was drawn back. The gun was cocked. Rawlings' finger was on the trigger, crooked.

"He's going to kill her," I whispered, not turning my head.

"I think so, too," Friedman replied. "She isn't giving him any other way out. She's saving the kid—because she hates the man. They're crazy. Both of them."

"If he fires, we've got to fire, too."

"I know."

"You agree?"

He momentarily hesitated. Then, in a low voice, awed-sounding but very precise, he said, "Yes." Having said it, he was clearing his throat, once, twice, three times.

"Get ready, Harrington," I said. "When he fires at her—if he fires—you shoot. Aim at the base of his throat. Don't wait for my command. He fires, you fire. Immediately. Instantaneously. Otherwise, he'll kill the boy, too. Understood?"

"Y—yessir. Understood. I—"

"It's time for another step, Dave," she was saying. "This is the second one that I wasn't supposed to take. Or maybe it's the third; I lost track. Anyhow, I'm going to walk right up to you, one step at a time, and I'm going to take that big black toy of yours away from you." Slowly she stepped across the yellow dividing line. "And then, when I've taken it away, I'm going to—"

The automatic roared, kicking in the man's hand. The woman's body bucked, doubled over, thrown back, already crumpled, broken. Beside me, the rifle cracked, once. Caught at the neck and jerked from his feet, Rawlings crashed against the bridge railing, arms thrown out, legs wide apart, grotesquely spread-eagled. The boy was sinking slowly to his knees, staring with dark, round eyes at his mother's twitching, blood-blotched body. The boy looked as if he were praying.

"You check the woman," I said. "I'll check Rawlings."

Without waiting for a reply, I was walking toward the railing, my gun held ready. As I moved toward him, Rawlings slowly slumped to a sitting position, propped against the railing. His legs were still spread. His head lolled. His arms were limp at his sides. At the base of his neck a bright red stain was spreading across the dark blue nylon of his jacket. His eyes were open, glazed, staring at nothing. He still held the gun with slack fingers. He was still alive.

With my gun aimed at his head, flanked by a half-dozen officers, I slowly approached the limp, bleeding man. His line of vision passed just above my head, but his eyes were empty.

Kneeling beside him, my gun now touching his temple, I reached for the barrel of the cocked automatic. Very carefully I withdrew the pistol from his hand. Holstering my revolver, I eased off the hammer of the Colt, then slipped the heavy gun into my jacket pocket.

Close around me, I was conscious of other men exhaling, straightening, uncocking their weapons, snapping their holster straps.

Still kneeling, I used thumb and forefinger to unzip Rawlings' jacket, careful not to touch the blood.

Harrington's shot had gone five inches wide. The .30-caliber bullet had torn through the big trapezius muscle just above the collarbone, striking at the angle of the neck and shoulder. Rawlings was only stunned, in deep shock. If the shot had gone an inch higher, it would have been a clean miss.

Straightening, I motioned for the ambulance stewards standing by. Then I turned toward the small group surrounding Jane Swanson. Meeting my eye, Friedman shook his head.

The boy was on his feet, swaying, stumbling toward the blanket-covered shape at Friedman's feet.

24

"To show you that there's no hard feelings about the great jogging conspiracy," Friedman said, sinking gratefully into my visitor's chair, "I thought I'd show you this. Prepublication, you might say." He tossed a slim sheaf of foolscap sheets haphazardly across my desk.

"What is it?"

"My report on your war with Howard Draper. It'll probably make you famous—a departmental celebrity."

"If it's that good, I probably couldn't improve on it."

He extracted a slightly bent cigar from his inside pocket. Frowning, he straightened it. "You don't *have* to read it, of course. If I were you, in fact, I think I'd go home. For a week."

"I haven't finished my report on Rawlings."

"Is he still confessing to anyone who'll listen?"

"About the murders, yes. But he still won't say whether he robbed Valenti."

"Maybe it was a crime of pure passion."

"That's a lot of it. But whenever he's asked about torturing Valenti, he looks a little wall-eyed. And he denies the robbery too loudly—like he's shocked at the mere suggestion."

"He's probably got the loot stashed somewhere, for his old age."

"Maybe." I was moodily fingering a pack of cigarettes I kept on the desk, testing the strength of my no-smoking resolution.

"How'd he actually commit the murder?"

"About like I had it figured. He got in through the front service entrance, then went along the side of the house. He jimmied the back door, then just walked in on them, waving the gun. He says they were making love and didn't hear him until he was right in the room with them. And, apparently, the fact that they were making love pushed him over the edge. He kept talking about the naked woman. Every time he mentioned her, he got a kind of wild glint in his eye, like he was one of those nutty revivalists preaching against sin."

"Are you saying he's a nut?"

"No. Not certifiable, anyhow. In fact, he's pretty plausible-sounding most of the time—pretty lucid. He claims that he originally intended just to scare Valenti—warn him to stay away from Jane. It turns out that Jane did phone Valenti, after all. She made the call the minute Rawlings was out of the apartment. He listened from the hallway, and heard her talking—hitting Valenti for money, because she wanted to leave Rawlings and go back to Los Angeles. That's when Rawlings decided to do the job. It was a spur-of-the-moment decision, even though he'd obviously already done some planning."

"Were they sleeping together—Jane and Valenti? Was that what really bugged Rawlings?"

"I don't think so. I think she used Valenti like a whip. She was one of these man-eating women."

"Most hookers are. Their one true love is their pimp—because he beats them. It's a father thing, according to my son the psychology student." He drew thoughtfully, slowly, on the cigar, then said, "Personally, I think robbery was at least a secondary motive. A hot-blooded lover acting in the heat of passion doesn't plan a month ahead of time to steal a car for the job."

"Exactly. That's the way I put it to him, too."

"What'd he say?"

"He didn't say anything. Essentially, he's just telling us what he wants us to hear."

"Did he steal the car because he wanted to throw suspicion on Bruce Manley?"

"No. That was pure coincidence. He doesn't even know Bruce

Manley exists. As Kreiger said, there're thousands of white Volks-wagens around."

"Coincidence is very tough on cops," Friedman observed. "What'd he do after he walked in during their sex scene?"

"He's not really sure," I answered slowly, "and I believe him. The only thing that's really clear is that, first, he had Karen tie Valenti to the bedpost. Then he tortured Valenti, while she watched. Then he shot Valenti. He didn't shoot the girl until he was ready to leave, I don't think."

"And he did it all because of unrequited love," Friedman rumbled ironically. "Sometimes I think there're almost as many people slaughtered in the name of true love as there are in the name of the one true God." He glanced wearily at his watch. "Well, it's eight o'clock, and my wife's still keeping dinner warm. These days, it takes longer to write the report than it does to catch the bad guys. In my youth, it was a duplicate society. Now it's a triplicate society. And before long—"

My phone rang.

"This is Canelli, Lieutenant. I'm down in the garage, where the lab boys are working on Rawlings' car. And guess what?"

"I give up, Canelli. What?"

"They found almost eighteen thousand dollars wired to the frame of Rawlings' car, up over the differential. All in used tens and twenties. I bet it'll turn out to be the Valenti money."

"I wouldn't be surprised. You can bring it up here, along with one lab man as witness. I'll give you a receipt and have it put in the safe."

"Check."

"What about Jane Swanson's boy?"

I could hear him sigh. "He's over at Youth Guidance. And the hell of it is, Draper's little girl's there, too. Christ, two orphans in one day. It makes you think."

"I've just been talking to Judge Walker and Susan Draper's parents. They'll be able to get the little girl tomorrow." I hesitated, then asked, "How's she doing, would you say?"

Again he sighed. "I'd say she isn't doing very good, Lieutenant.

She keeps saying that she knows her daddy didn't kill her mommy, because her daddy loved her mommy."

"I suppose he did, once."

"Yeah."

"What about Jane Swanson's kid? How'd he take it?"

"Well, he didn't say much. He just sat staring at me—like he was accusing me, or something. He's a real strange kid—like a small, shrunken little man, or something. I bet he never laughs."

"He's probably never had much to laugh about."

"Yeah, I guess you're right." He paused. "I'm sorry I took so long over at Youth Guidance. I—you know—I got bogged down, I guess you'd say."

"That's all right, Canelli. Bring that money up. I'm going home pretty soon."

"Right."

I hung up and swiveled to face Friedman.

"Don't tell me," he said, holding up a warning hand. "Canelli found the loot. By accident."

"Wrong. The lab boys found it. Eighteen thousand dollars."

"The way Bruce Manley and Billy Mitchell were talking," he said absently, "Valenti and the girl probably stashed the money under their pillow, so they wouldn't have to leave bed even to make change for their drug customers." He flicked his cigar ash, missing my ashtray. His eyes had a faraway look. "I wonder what they do at Youth Guidance Center for Christmas," he said finally, staring impassively down at his cigar.

"They pass out presents to the little kids—the ones under twelve." I sailed his report across the desk. "Here—you proofread it. I've got my own report to do."

He shrugged, collected the papers and slowly got to his feet. "You never did tell me what you're doing for Christmas, much less Hanukkah."

"It just so happens," I said, walking with him to the door, "that I got an invitation for Christmas dinner, just an hour ago. From a very pretty lady. For Hanukkah, I'm coming to your house."

He nodded, opening the door. "Good. Who's the pretty lady?"

"The mother of one of our ex-suspects, Ann Haywood. She's an admirer of good police work, I guess."

He snorted. "She's probably got a thing about aging football players." He looked me up and down, frowning reflectively. "You're beaming like a schoolboy," he said finally. "Maybe you should bring her for Hanukkah."

"Maybe I will."

ABOUT THE AUTHOR

COLLIN WILCOX *was born in Detroit, Michigan,
educated at Antioch College, and served in the
Air Corps before settling down to live in San
Francisco, where he moonlights as a retailer of
lamps. His hobbies are bridge, poker and vintage
airplanes, and he is a conservationist and wildlife
observer.*